- HERGÉ -

TINTIN'S LAST ADVENTURE

TINTIN
AND
ALPH-ART

Ⓛ Ⓑ
LITTLE, BROWN AND COMPANY
New York Boston

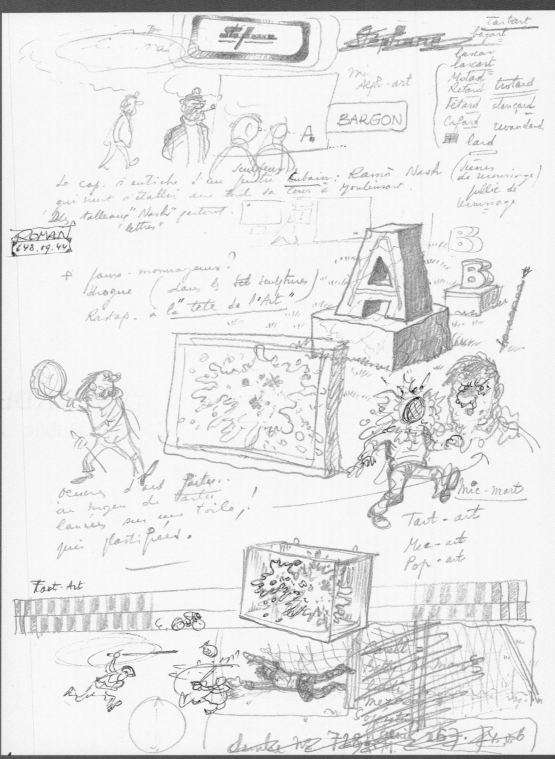

BARGON
Tart-art
Mic-mart
Pop-art

Translated by Leslie Lonsdale-Cooper and Michael Turner

www.casterman.com
www.tintin.com

Published pursuant to agreement with Editions Casterman, Tournai.
Not for sale in the British Commonwealth.

Little, Brown and Company
Hachette Book Group
237 Park Avenue, New York, NY 10017
Visit our website at www.lb-teens.com

Little, Brown and Company is a division of Hachette Book Group, Inc.
The Little, Brown name and logo are trademarks of Hachette Book Group, Inc.
First Paperback Edition: December 2007
ISBN-13 : 978-0-316-00375-9
10 9 8 7 6
Printed in China

Tintin – the last adventure

Tintin was born from the pencil and pen of Hergé seventy-five years ago. He lives today in the collective imagination of millions of readers for whom, in the most ordinary or the most unexpected circumstances, come reminders of one moment or another of his adventures – immediate, spontaneous, heart-warming.

Hergé's final creation began in 1978 and remains unfinished: he worked on *Alph-Art* not knowing where the story would lead. He left more than an outline, a little less than an adventure, but so many possibilities, so many flights of imagination, so many dreams.

In 1986, a lavish album reproduced in facsimile the principal sketches from this work in progress.

Today, like a gift for Tintin's seventy-fifth birthday, *Alph-Art* has been given an entirely new presentation. The format and the pagination, just like the other albums, are familiar. The layout, with its excellent legibility, enhances the drawings, the roughs, the sketches, with an ease of access that draws the reader ever more closely into the story.

The last pages – a series of unpublished documents recently discovered – shed entirely fresh light on the 'incomplete conclusion' of the story.

Marlinspike Hall...

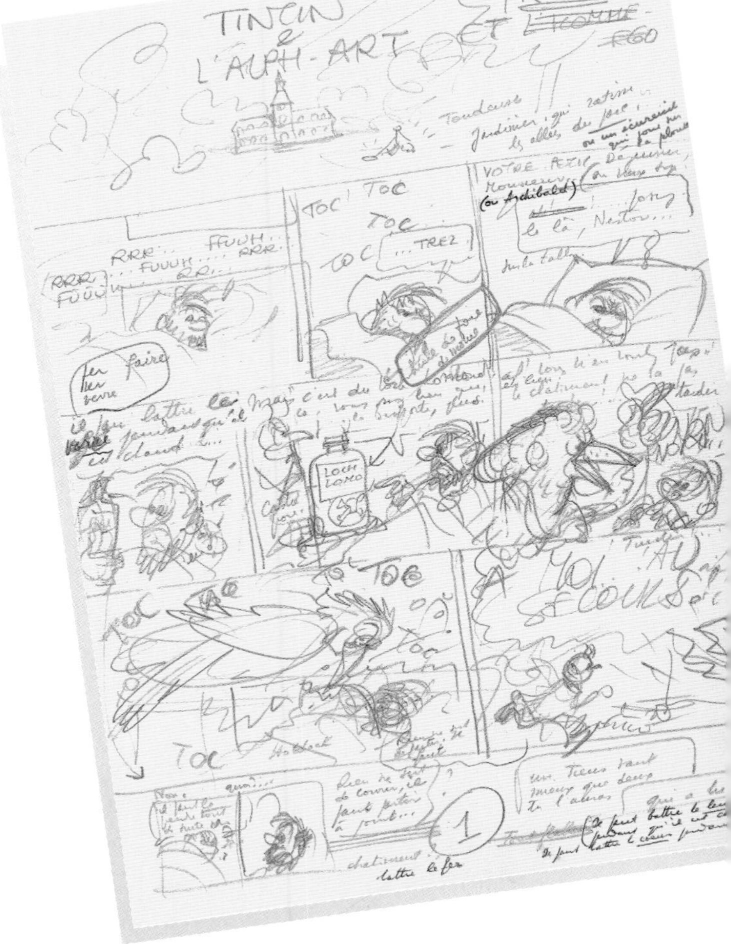
TINTIN
&
L'ALPH-ART
ROMEO
TOC TOC
TOC
LOCH
LOMO
1

Marlinspike Hall, one fine summer morning. Everything seems at peace in the great park surrounding the house. Outside the windows of the bedroom where Captain Haddock is fast asleep, a green woodpecker is hammering away at a tree-trunk. Still not awake, the Captain thinks someone is knocking at his door. He sighs.

HADDOCK: Mmm... Mmm?... Yes?... Come in...
A VOICE: Your breakfast, Captain.
HADDOCK: Let me sleep, Nestor...
THE VOICE: Out of the question. You must take your medicine.

Astonished, the Captain opens his eyes. This isn't Nestor! Bianca Castafiore, more bossy than ever, has come into the room. And instead of breakfast, she carries a bottle of whisky labelled with a skull and crossbones.

HADDOCK: But that's Loch Lomond, Signora... You know very well I can't stand it any more.

But as Signora Castafiore approaches the Captain, she turns into a strange bird, part chicken, part woodpecker.

THE CASTAFIORE BIRD: Oh, so you don't want it... In that case you can't have any pudding.

And turning completely into a bird, she begins to peck at the unfortunate Captain.

HADDOCK: Help! Help! Save me!

The awful shrieks have woken Tintin. He rushes to the Captain's room.

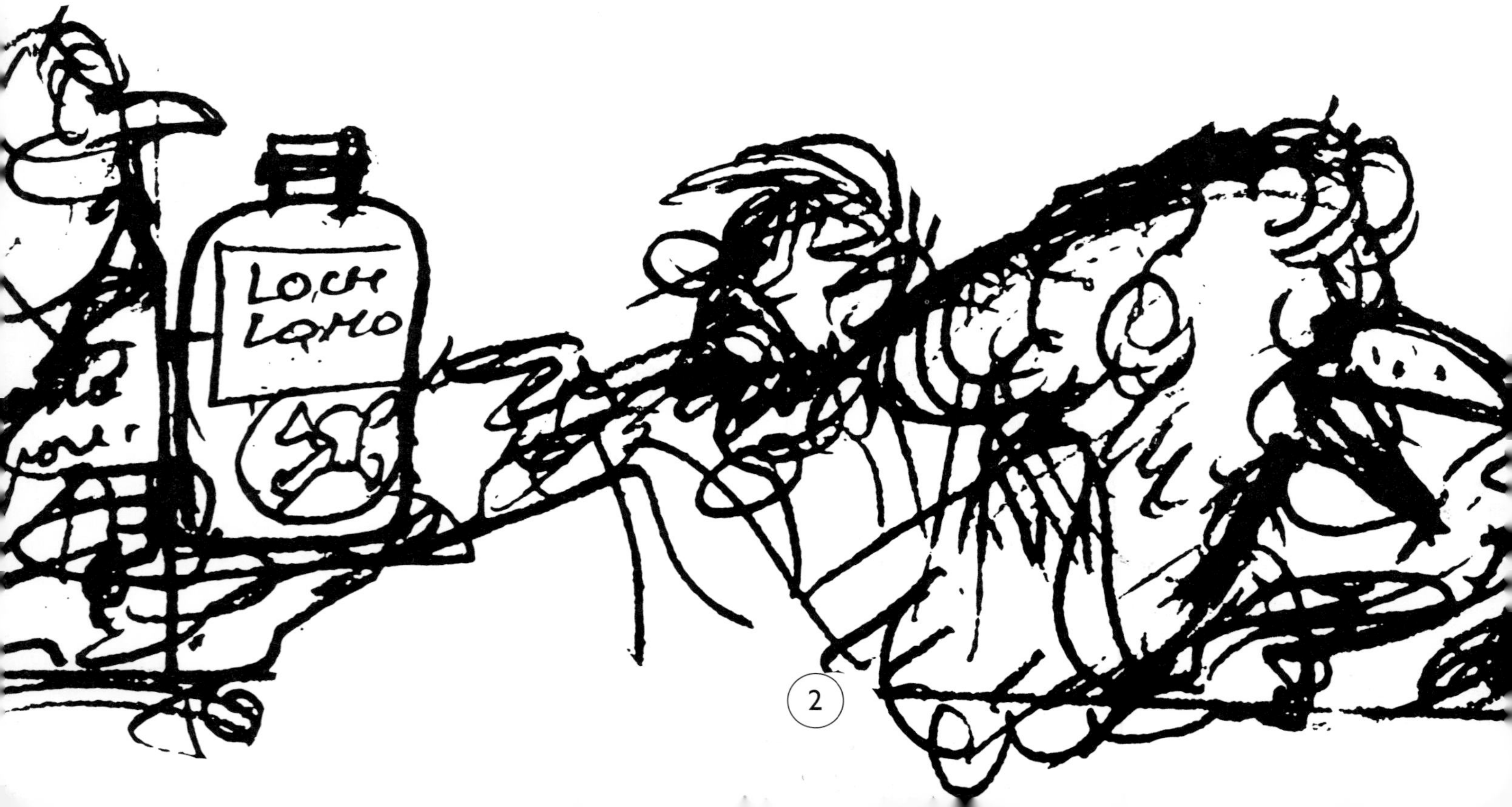
LOCH
LOMO

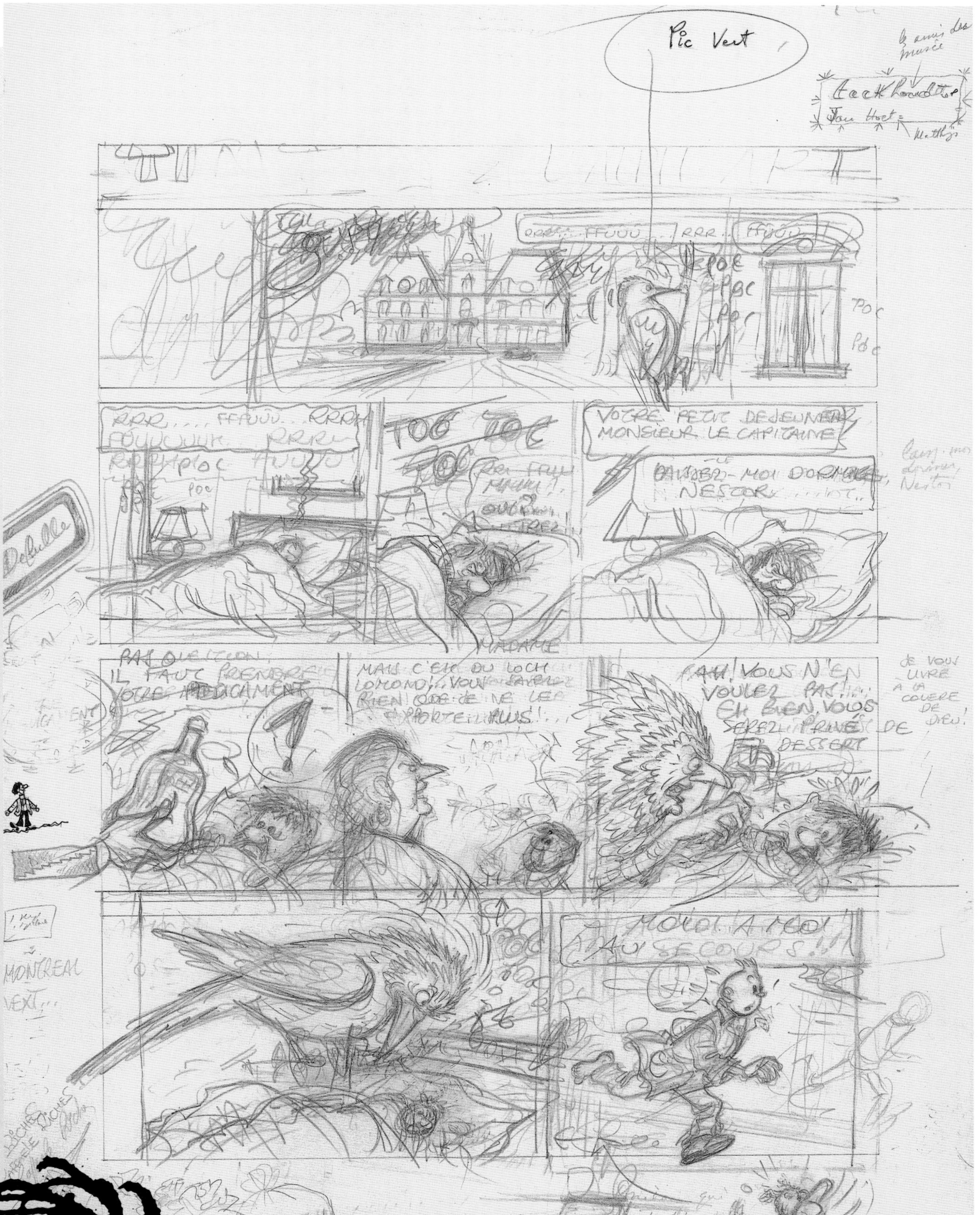
Pic Vert
RRR... FFUUU...
POC POC POC
VOTRE PETIT DEJEUNER MONSIEUR LE CAPITAINE
LAISSEZ-MOI DORMIR NESTOR...
IL FAUT PRENDRE VOTRE MEDICAMENT
MAIS C'EST DU LOCH LOMOND!...
AH! VOUS N'EN VOULEZ PAS!... EH BIEN, VOUS SEREZ PRIVÉ DE DESSERT
A MOI! A MOI! AU SECOURS!!

Still lost in his nightmare, the Captain continues to defend himself against his imaginary attacker.

HADDOCK: No! No! No!

TINTIN: Captain!

Thrashing about, the Captain half stuns Tintin who is trying to wake him. Then reality dawns; he opens his eyes and comes to his senses. He sits up.

HADDOCK: Oh… Good heavens! But… Tintin… What are you doing here?... What a nightmare! What a horrible nightmare!... Just imagine…

The telephone starts to ring. Tintin answers it.

TINTIN: Hello? Yes!... No, madam, you have the wrong number… No, this is not Mr Cutts the butcher! Not at all, madam.

HADDOCK: As I was telling you, a horrible nightmare… There was Nestor bringing my breakfast. But it wasn't Nestor, and it wasn't my breakfast either.

TINTIN: Oh yes?...

HADDOCK: Then suddenly…

Once again the telephone rings, interrupting the Captain.

TINTIN: Again?... *(He picks up the telephone)* Hello? Yes… Wh-wh-… what?... Who? Signora Castafiore?

HADDOCK: No! It can't be true!!!

CASTAFIORE: Yes, I've just arrived from Los Angeles… Yes… And I'm in your country for two days. I'm planning to come and embrace you, you and my brave Hassock. How is the dear man?

TINTIN: Very well, Signora, I… He's just gone out!... He will be so upset to have missed you…

CASTAFIORE: Tomorrow, then… Oh, no! Tomorrow is impossible!... I have a date with Endaddine!

TINTIN: Endaddine?

CASTAFIORE: Don't tell me you don't know Endaddine? The great, the one and only Endaddine Akass! He is a fascinating man, darling, absolutely fascinating. You simply must meet him. He's the most m-a-a-rvellous mystic… He lays his hands on your head and you're magnetised for a year. In fact, I'm going to spend a few days with him… You absolutely have to meet him… He's inspired. But I must leave you now, I'm going window-shopping. Lots of kisses to my dear Paddock. Ciao!

TINTIN: Goodbye, Signora.

He hangs up with relief, and hurries into the passageway in pursuit of the Captain.

TINTIN: Captain! Hey, Captain!

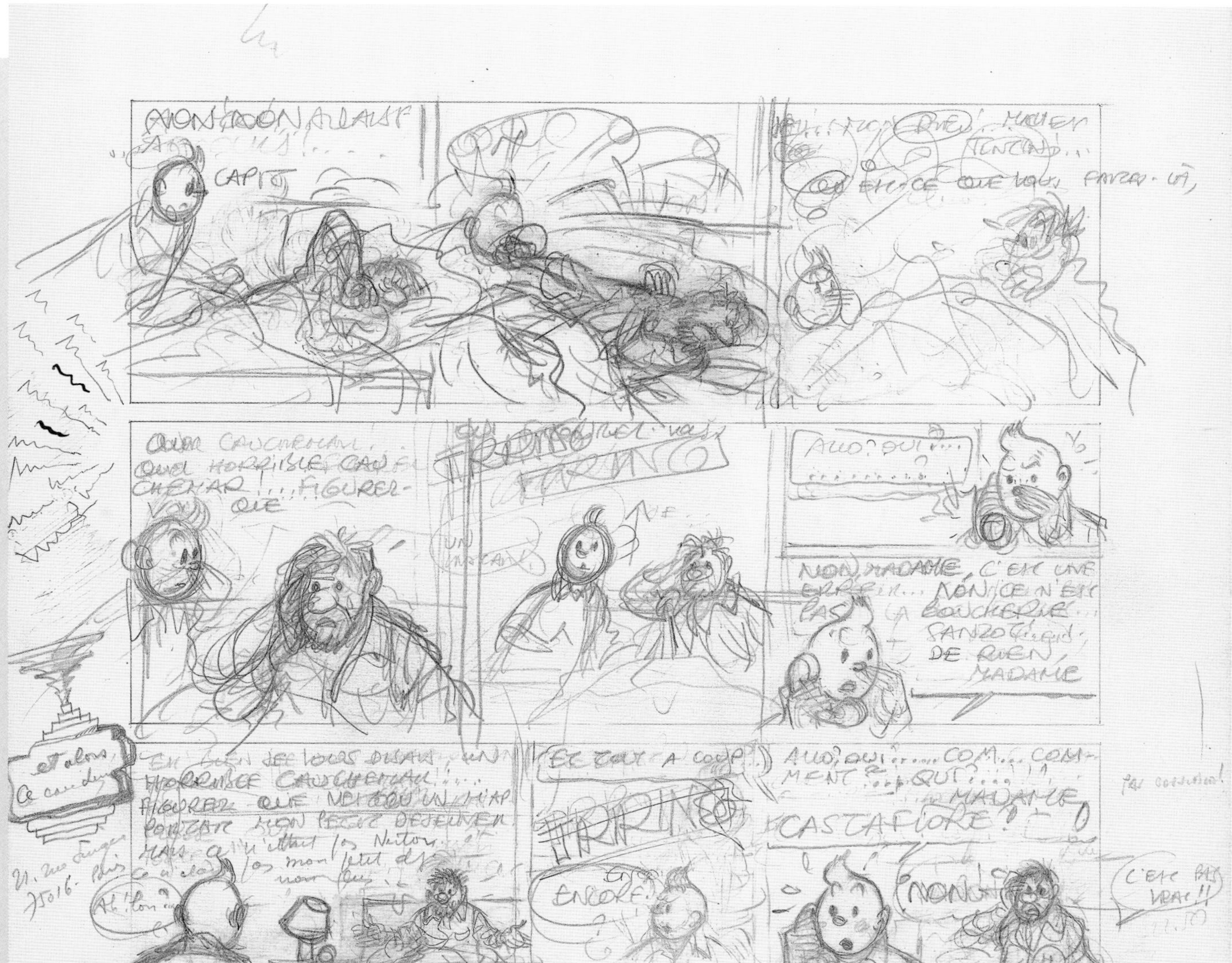
CAPIT...
ALLO? OUI...?
NON MADAME, C'EST UNE ERREUR... NON, CE N'EST PAS LA BOUCHERIE SANZOT... DE RIEN, MADAME
ENCORE!
ALLO, OUI... COM... COMMENT?... QUI?... MADAME CASTAFIORE?
NON!
C'EST PAS VRAI!!
OUI, J'ARRIVE DE LOS ANGELES...
TRES BIEN, MADAME, JE... IL VIENT JUSTEMENT DE SORTIR... IL SERA DESOLE DE VOUS AVOIR MANQUE...
TELEPHONEZ-VOUS?
DE L'AEROPORT, TRES CHER!
Tourniquet
Tournebroche
Tournedisque
Tournedos

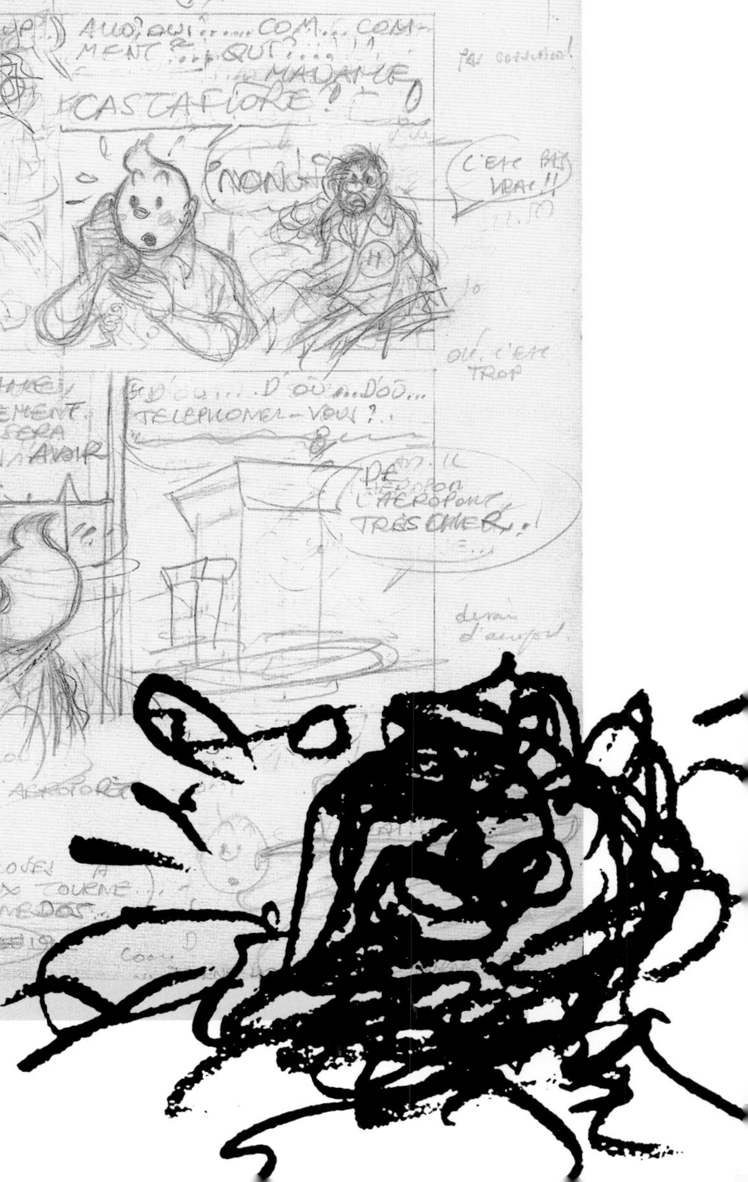

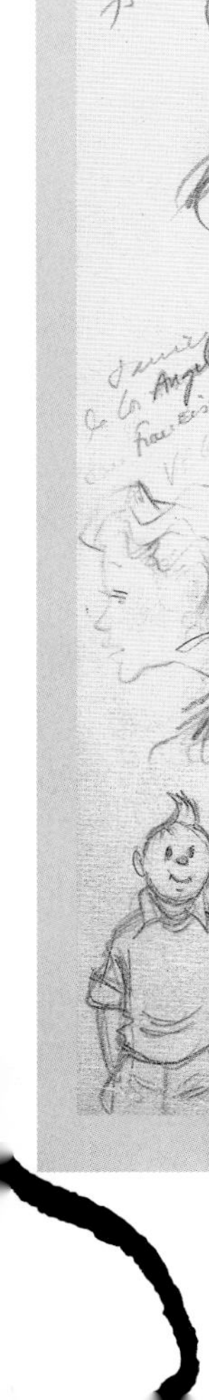

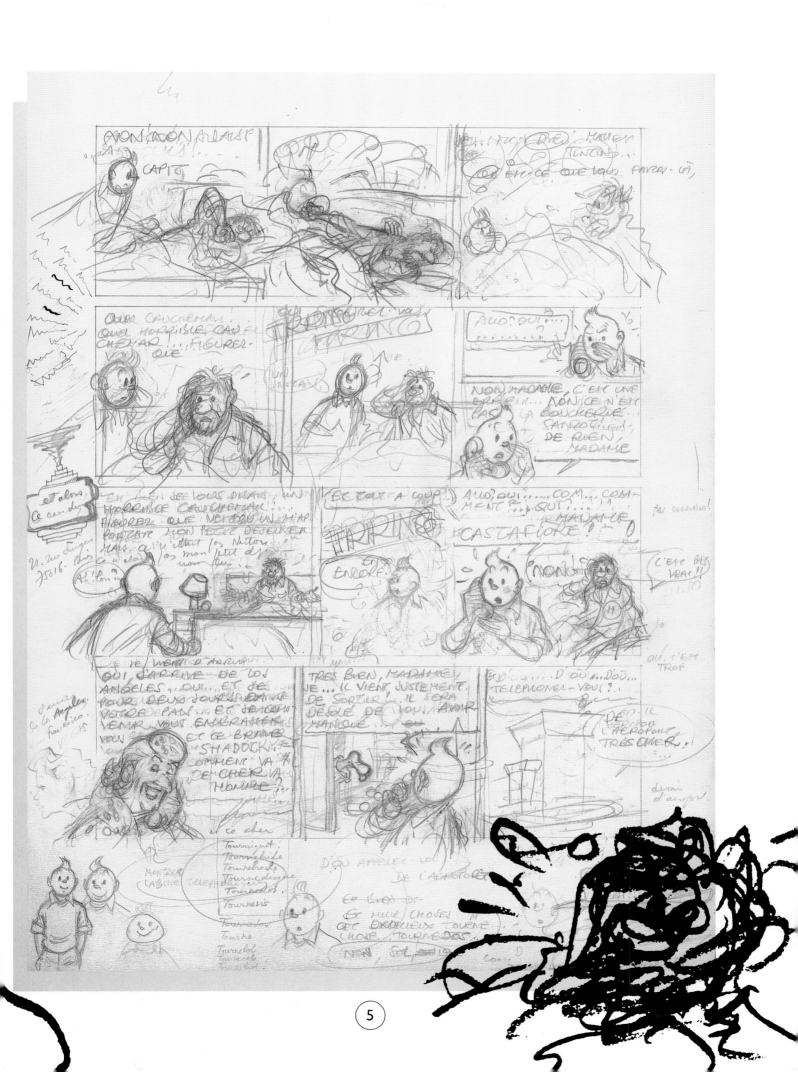

The Fourcart Gallery...

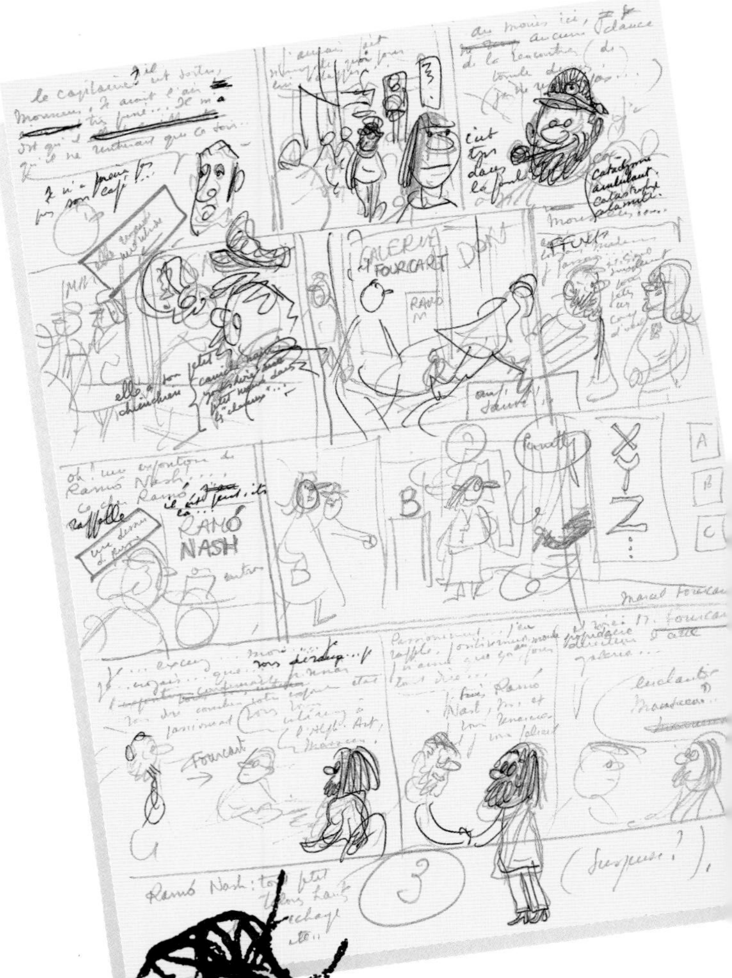
FOURCART
RAMÓ NASH

NESTOR: The Captain? He went out, sir. He seemed in a great hurry. He didn't even drink his coffee. He said he wouldn't be back until this evening.

TINTIN: Oh?... Right!

In a busy street in the centre of town, the Captain is strolling along, smoking his pipe.

HADDOCK: Yes, there's nothing I wouldn't do to escape her! Ha! ha! Lost in the crowd, here in town, I'm out of danger!

Suddenly, Castafiore comes sailing round the corner, a miniature poodle in her arms and Igor Wagner, her accompanist, at her heels.

HADDOCK: Catastrophe! Cataclysm! Calamity! Good heavens, what can I do? What can I do?

To avoid the diva, the Captain dashes into the nearest doorway, the Fourcart Gallery.

HADDOCK: Phew! Saved!

An assistant with enormous spectacles advances towards him.

THE ASSISTANT: Can I help you, sir?

HADDOCK: Good morning... I was just passing... Just thought I'd look around...

Castafiore also comes past the gallery. Suddenly she sees in the window a poster displaying the name of Ramó Nash.

CASTAFIORE: Oh! An exhibition of Ramó Nash... Dearest Ramó... I'm wild about him... Perhaps he's there... Let's go in!

She goes into the gallery, flanked by her ever-present accompanist. Panic-stricken, the Captain rushes into an adjoining room. Two men are sitting at a table. The first, quite short, has long hair, a scarf and a thick pullover. The second seems more of a businessman.

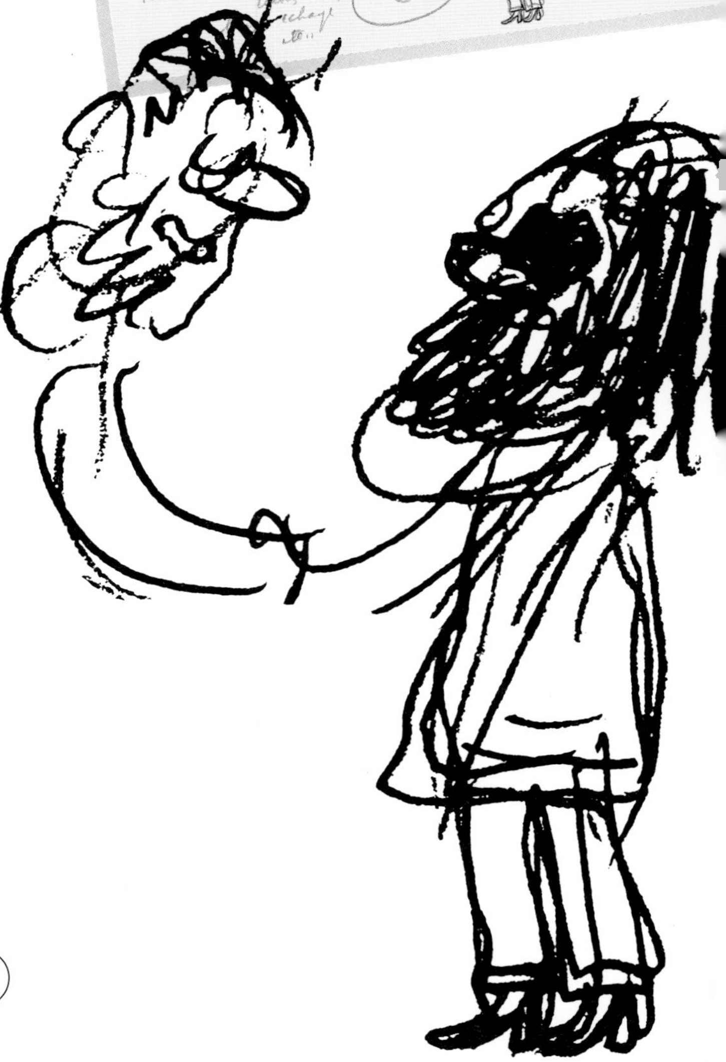

HADDOCK: I... Excuse me... I'm disturbing you... I thought... I wanted to tell you how fascinating I find your exhibition.

THE LITTLE MAN: You are interested in Alph-Art, sir?

HADDOCK: Passionately... I'm absolutely wild about it... Nothing I like better, that's for sure.

THE LITTLE MAN: I am Ramó Nash, sir. I thank you, and I congratulate you. And this is Mr Fourcart, the director of the gallery.

FOURCART: How do you do, Mr... Mr...?

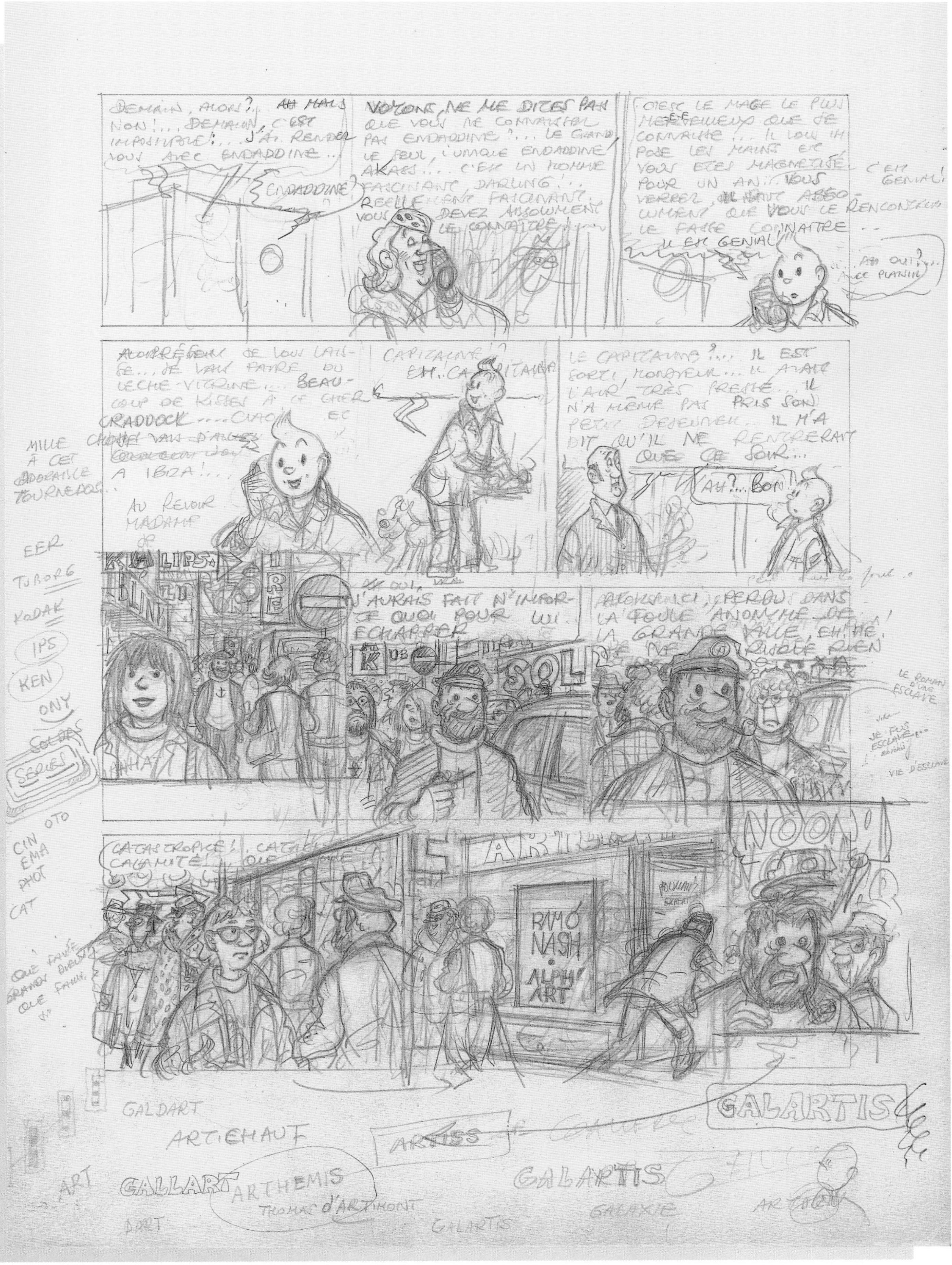
ENDADDINE ?
C'EST GÉNIAL!
AH?... BON!
LE CAPITAINE?... IL EST SORTI, MONSIEUR... IL AVAIT L'AIR TRÈS PRESSÉ... IL N'A MÊME PAS PRIS SON PETIT DÉJEUNER... IL M'A DIT QU'IL NE RENTRERAIT QUE CE SOIR...
CAPITAINE!
A IBIZA!...
AU REVOIR MADAME
MILLE ... À CET ADORABLE TOURNEDOS...
KODAK
KEN
ONY
SERIES
J'AURAIS FAIT N'IMPORTE QUOI POUR LUI ÉCHAPPER
SOL
LE ROMAN D'UNE ESCLAVE
VIE D'ESCLAVE
CATASTROPHE! CALAMITÉ!
NOON!
RAMÓ NASH • ALPH'ART
CIN ÉMA
PHOT
CAT
GALDART
ARTIEHAUT
ARTISS
GALARTIS
GALLART
ARTHEMIS
THOMAS D'ARTIMONT
GALARTIS
GALAXIE
GALARTIS

HADDOCK: Haddock… Archibald Haddock.

FOURCART: Haddock?... Not by any chance Tintin's greatest friend?

HADDOCK: That's me, yes.

FOURCART: H'm, h'm, h'mm. What a stroke of luck! Well, it so happens I have something interesting to tell him… Could I perhaps meet him one day?... As he is a journalist…

The assistant passes through the office, visibly interested.

HADDOCK: But, of course. I'll give you the telephone number of Marlinspike Hall. It's Marlinspike 621.

FOURCART: Good. Thank you very much. I'll leave you to go round the exhibition with Ramó Nash. I will telephone Tintin in a day or two.

RAMÓ NASH: This way, sir… *(The artist marches the Captain towards the gallery. At the foot of the staircase the two come face to face with Castafiore)* Dearest Bianca!

CASTAFIORE: Ramó!... Darling, what a surprise! My goodness me!

They embrace noisily, under the interested scrutiny of the assistant.

RAMÓ NASH: My dear friend, allow me to present an art lover…

CASTAFIORE: Captain Stopcock!... You here!... What a pleasure!

HADDOCK *(Despite his lack of enthusiasm, he cannot escape the singer's embraces)*: Bianca!... You here!... What a surprise!

CASTAFIORE: How delightful to find you here!... You're interested in Alph-Art!... Well! I'd never have thought it possible… That a simple fisherman, without any education, should be mad about art… It's fantastic! *(She turns towards Ramó Nash)* It proves that your art, so simple and at the same time so rich, so noble and so basic, can reach the whole world… from the most uncouth to the most… the most… Well, to people like us… Ah, Alph-Art! A genuine return to the sources, to the caves of Castamura… er, of Lascaux… well, in a nutshell, it is the art of our time. In it we return to the origins of civilisation, don't we?

The wheel, fire, the hard-boiled egg… and goodness knows what else!... It is inspired, my dear Ramó, inspired! *(She stops before a sort of lamp-stand surmounted by a small sphere)* Look at that, Captain Kapok! What strength, what nobility! You feel better when you've seen that, don't you?

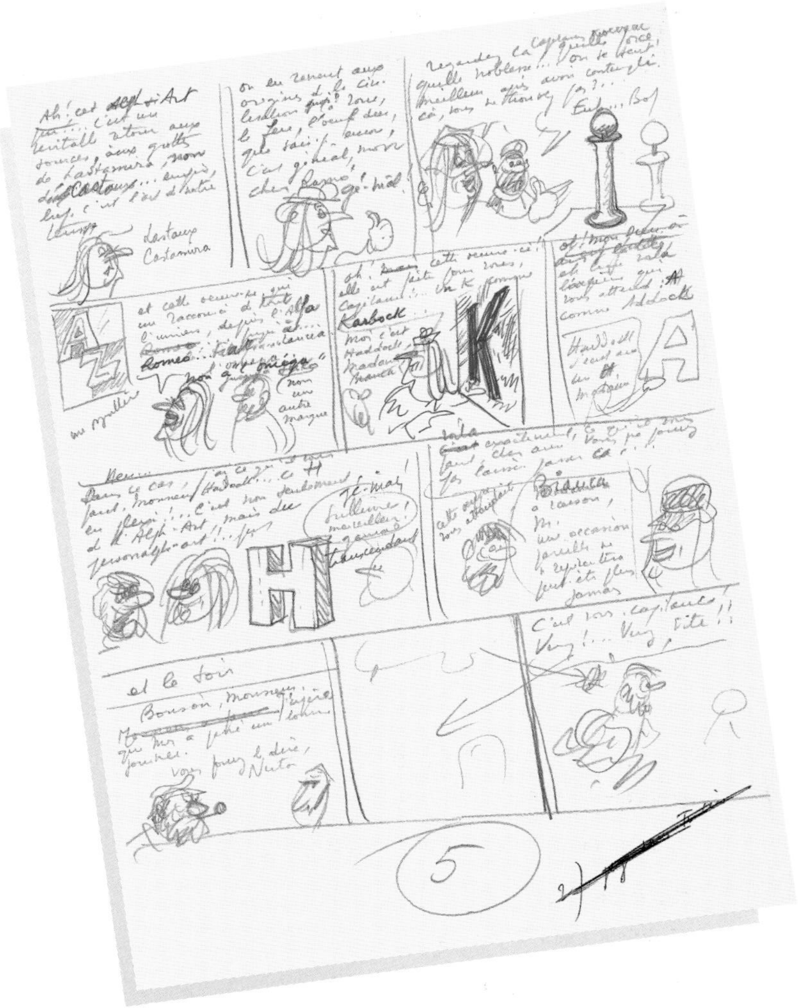

HADDOCK: Er… Um…

Castafiore has already taken the Captain up to another Ramó Nash creation, a picture displaying, in capitals, the letters A and Z.

CASTAFIORE: This work here, look! A microcosm of the whole universe, from Alfa to Romeo… Fiat… Lancia… to Omega… No, that's another make.

HADDOCK: Er…

CASTAFIORE *(Catches sight of another picture, showing a huge K)*: Oh, this one! Especially for you, Captain… K for Kapok!

HADDOCK: My name is Haddock, Signora Bianca.

CASTAFIORE: Oh, goodness! What am I thinking of? *(She spots another canvas)* Well, there's just the picture, waiting for you: A for Addock!

HADDOCK: Haddock is spelt with an H, Signora!

RAMÓ NASH: In that case, I have precisely what you need… This H in Perspex… Not just Alph-Art, but Personalph-Art!

CASTAFIORE: Inspired… Sublime… Marvellous… Transcendent!... It's exactly what you need, dear friend! You can't let it go: this piece was waiting for you.

RAMÓ NASH: Bianca is right, sir. Such a chance may never come your way again.

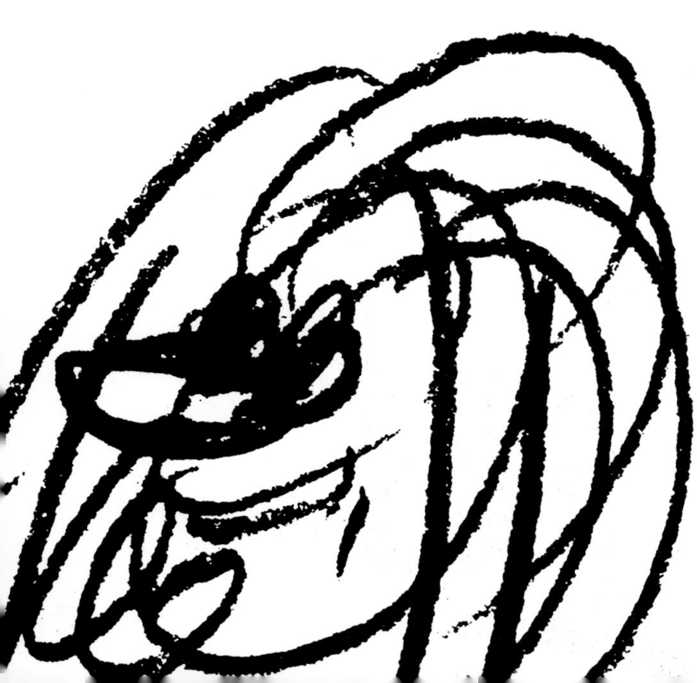

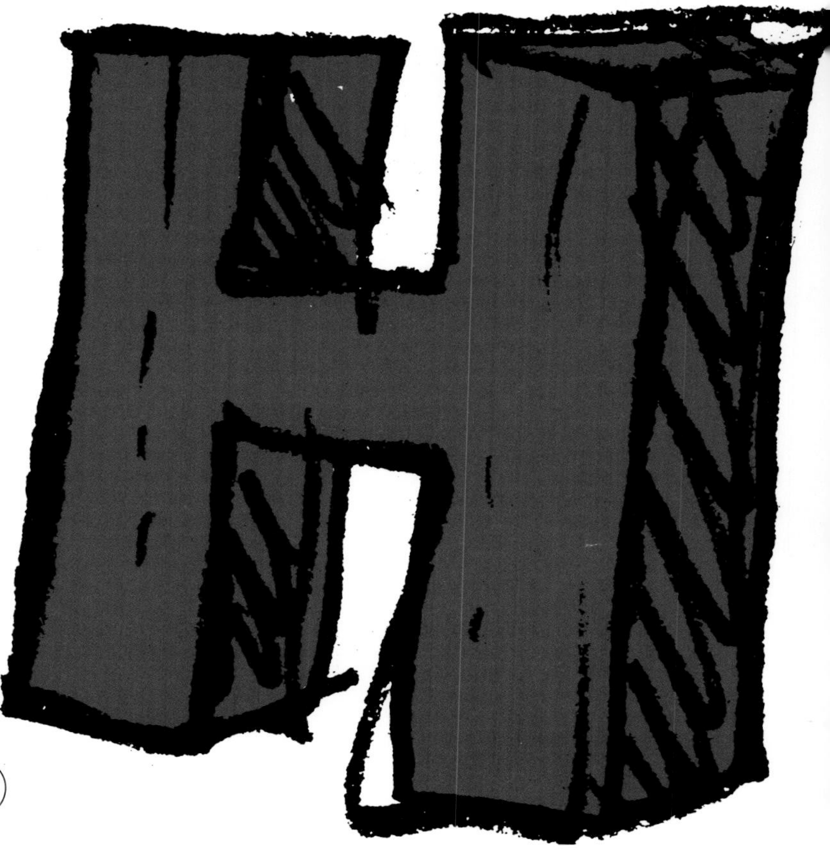

That evening, at Marlinspike...

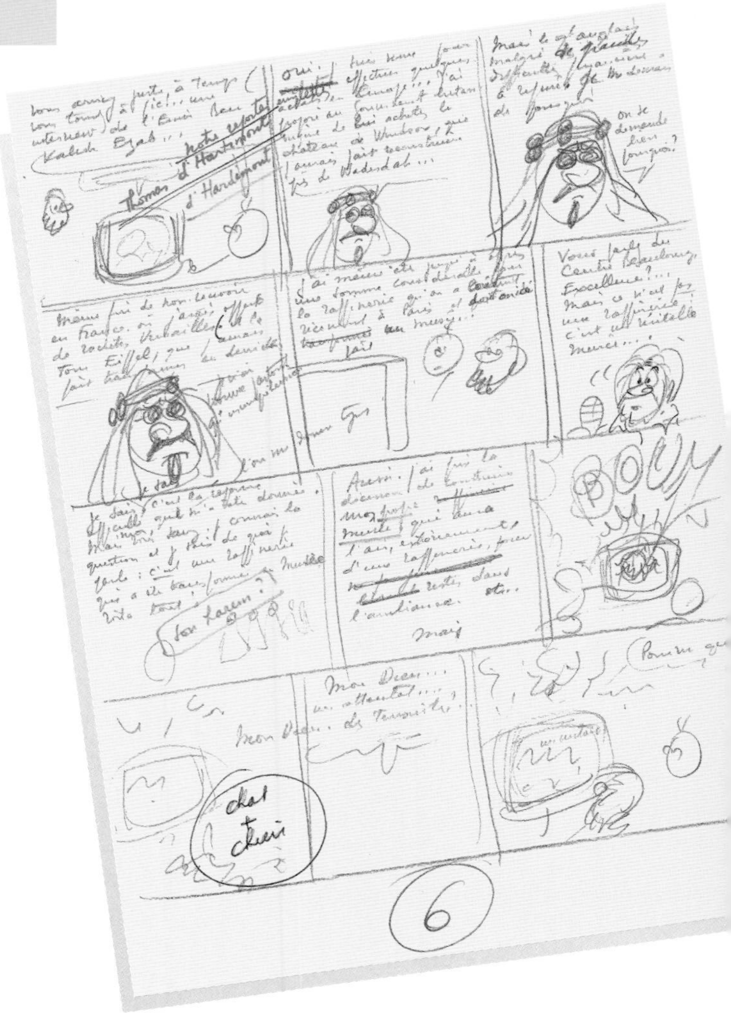

NESTOR: Good evening, sir, I hope you have had a good day.

HADDOCK *(exhausted, with a gloomy expression)*: You could say so, Nestor.

TINTIN *(off)*: Is that you, Captain? Here! Come quickly!

Haddock rushes into the drawing room.

TINTIN *(In front of the television, watching Ben Kalish Ezab being interviewed by Thomas d'Hartimont)*: You've come in time, exactly right… An interview with Emir Ben Kalish Ezab…

THE EMIR: Yes, I came to Europe to do a little shopping… I've offered to buy Windsor Castle from the British government, so I can put it up outside Wadesdah… But the British government refused, despite their great financial difficulties. One wonders why? The same brush-off in France, when I proposed to buy Versailles… And the Eiffel Tower, which I'd have converted to a derrick. Everywhere I was met with incomprehension. I was just about to offer a considerable sum for the refinery they built recently in Paris, and then used as a museum…

D'HARTIMONT *(with a start)*: You mean the Beaubourg Centre, Excellency?...

THE EMIR: I know, I know… That's the official story they gave me. But I can tell you, it's my line, and I know what I'm talking about: it *is* a refinery turned into a museum, and that's that! Now I've decided to build my own museum looking like a refinery on the outside, just to keep up with the fashion, but…

A violent explosion interrupts the Emir. Snowy and the cat, asleep in front of the television, leap up in panic.

TINTIN: Great snakes!... A terrorist attack… Let's hope…

The smoke quickly clears. On the screen Abdullah can be seen beside his father.

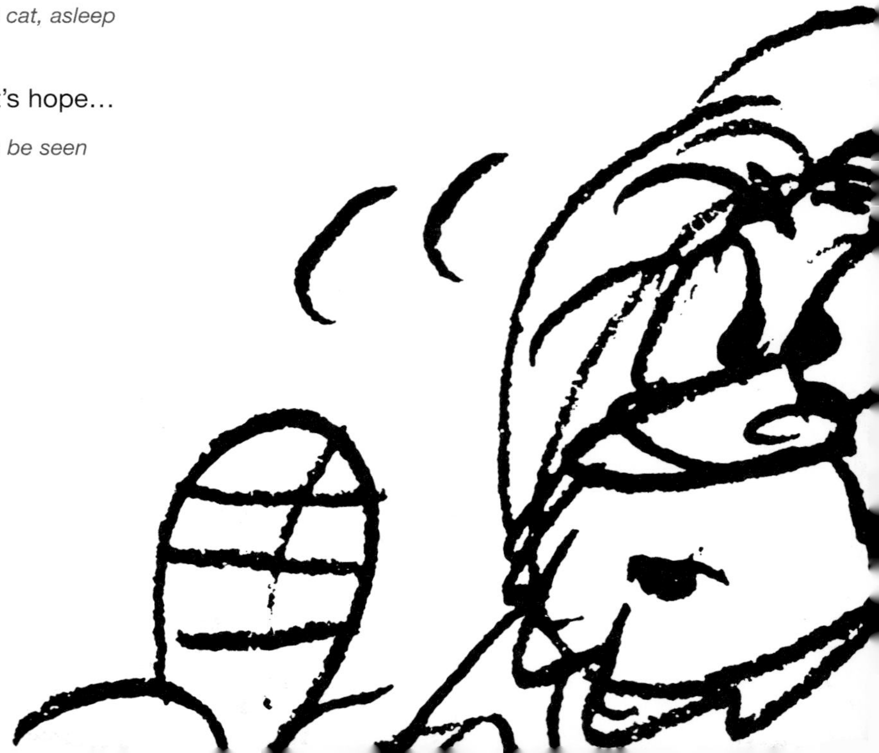

THE EMIR: Abdullah, my darling sugar-candy duckling… Aren't you ashamed of frightening the gentleman?

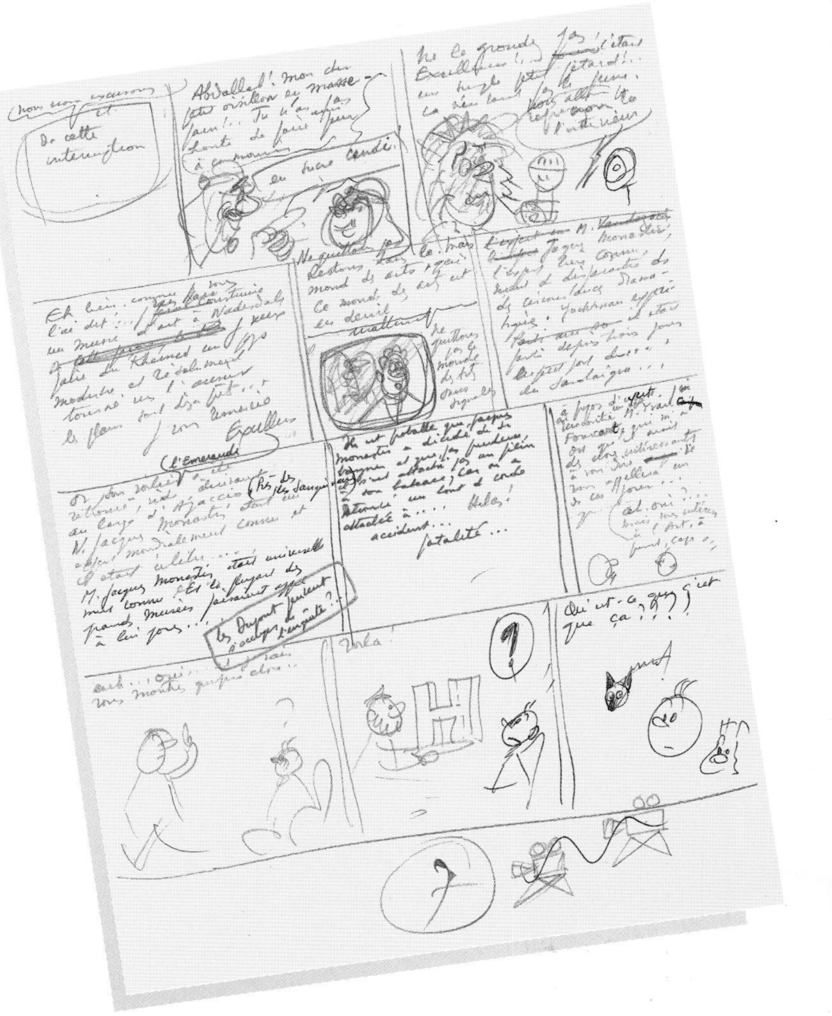

D'HARTIMONT: Don't scold him, Excellency. Think nothing of it. Just a little banger! Let's proceed with the interview.

THE EMIR: Well, as I was saying, I'm going to build a museum of Art at Wadesdah. I want to make Khemed into a modern country resolutely moving into the future. The plans are already drawn up.

D'HARTIMONT: Thank you, Your Excellency… And we stay with the world of art to report that Jacques Monastir, the well-known expert, has disappeared in dramatic circumstances. An experienced yachtsman, he left a small port in Sardinia three weeks ago. His yacht *Emerald* has been found empty, drifting off the Corsican coast at Ajaccio, near the Sanguinaires islands. A length of rope was attached to the boat. Jacques Monastir was known worldwide and most of the great museums called upon his expertise. It seems probable that Mr Monastir decided to go for a swim and, for safety, attached himself to the boat by a line. Then disaster must have struck.

HADDOCK: Talking of experts, I met a Mr Fourcart who told me he had something interesting to say to you. He'll ring you up some time…

TINTIN: Oh yes?... Are you getting interested in art, Captain?

HADDOCK: Er… yes… I mean… I've got something to show you…*(He fetches the large H in Perspex, bought that morning)* There!

TINTIN: Whatever's that?

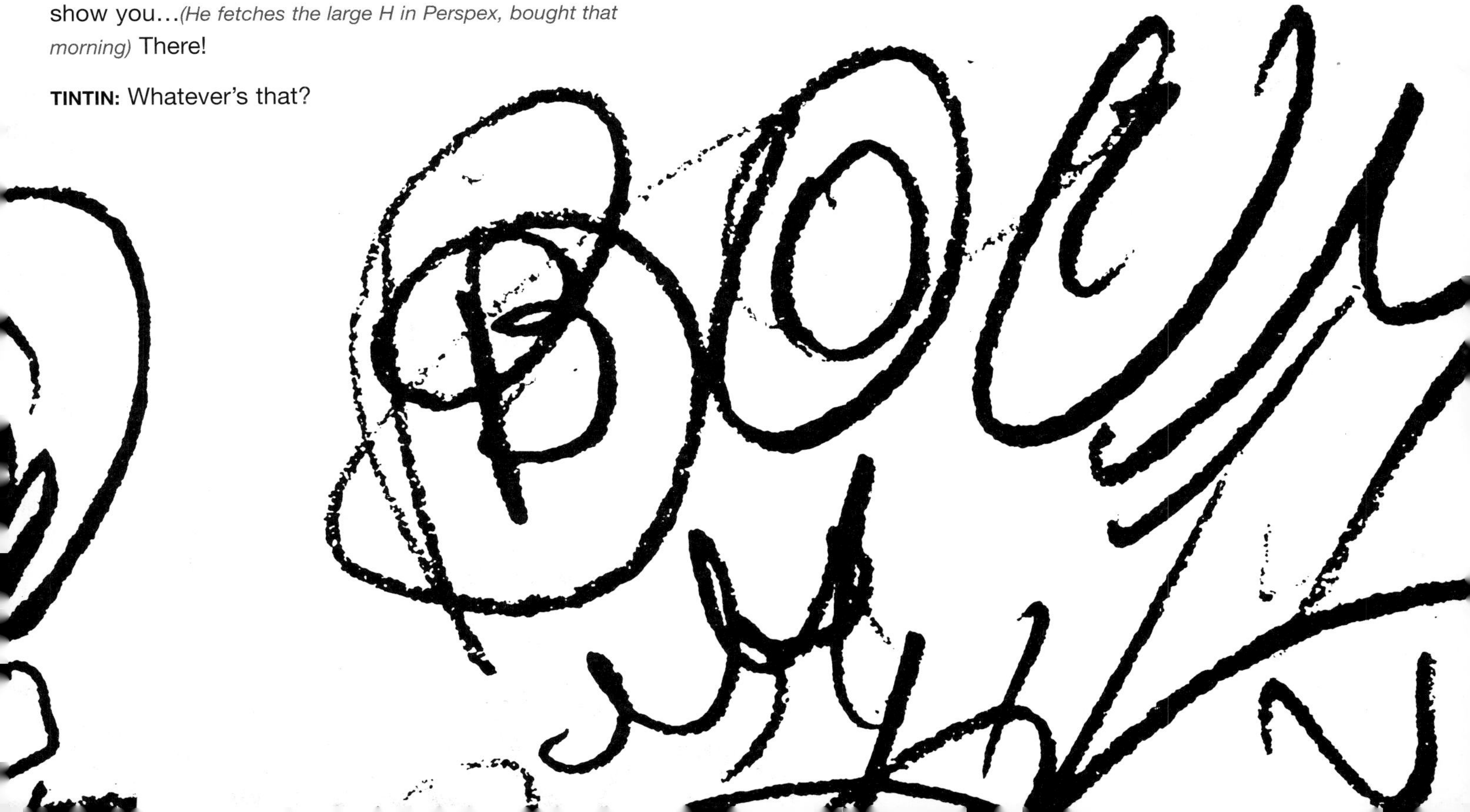

HADDOCK: It's Alph-Art, even Personalph-Art… H for HADDOCK, d'you get it?

TINTIN: I… Ah! Yes, er…

HADDOCK: And do you know, it's signed by Ramó Nash, the famous Jamaican artist… You've heard of him, haven't you?

TINTIN: Er, the name certainly rings a bell with me, but…

A familiar figure appears.

PROFESSOR CALCULUS: Hello, my friends.

HADDOCK: Cuthbert! How are you?

CALCULUS: A little chilly for the time of year, but still… Hello, what is that?

HADDOCK: That? That's a work by Ramó Nash.

CALCULUS: I can see perfectly well that it's an H, for goodness sake!… But what is it for?

HADDOCK: Nothing!… Nothing at all! It's a work of art! And a work of art isn't *for* anything! Art is art!

CALCULUS: A cart?… You are making fun of me, Captain!… I've had quite enough of that sort of joke…

HADDOCK: But…

CALCULUS: H for cart!… Really, what do you take me for?

HADDOCK: But Cuthbert, I… you…

TINTIN *(Picks up the object to look at it more closely)*: I… er… It's very nice, Captain… Most original…

HADDOCK: Isn't it? And… er… you know, when I saw that I was suddenly struck…

A door bell rings. Enter Thomson and Thompson, the certified detectives.

THE THOMPSONS: Good evening, everyone.

TINTIN: Good evening, gentlemen.

THOMSON: Goodness gracious! Where did that come from? It looks like an H. What is it for?

HADDOCK: It *is* an H. *(He is exasperated)* It isn't *for* anything!!! It's Alph-Art, that's all. And it isn't *for* anything!

THE THOMPSONS: Oh, good! Oh, well! Oh, good, good, good. Well, well.

HADDOCK: And what fair wind blows you here, gentlemen?

THOMSON: Well, it's like this!

THOMPSON: Yes, it's like this!

THOMSON: Perhaps you know that Emir Ben Kalish Ezab is on a visit to this country…

HADDOCK: Yes, we just saw him on television.

THOMPSON: Well, we have received certain information which makes us fear a terrorist attack upon him.

HADDOCK: Really?

THOMSON: Yes, it's feared that he may be kidnapped by a Palestinian commando.

HADDOCK: Really?

THOMPSON: So, we thought that perhaps, since you know him well, you might put him up here, incognito, him and his son. *(He offers a Havana to the Captain and to his colleague, and helps himself)* A cigar, Captain?

HADDOCK: Thanks… My dear friends *(Puff!)*, I should be happy to accommodate *(Puff!)* an entire tribe of Carpathian bashi-bazouks, or even *(Puff, puff!)* a herd of fully-grown buffalo *(Puff!)*, but have young Abdullah here? Never again!… Never again!

THOMPSON: But he's the nicest little boy in the world… These cigars we're smoking, he gave them to us himself.

THOMSON: That was kind, wasn't it?

HADDOCK: You think so? Well, if I were you I'd watch out, because that little brat…

A double BANG interrupts him. The Thompsons' cigars have exploded, one after another.

12

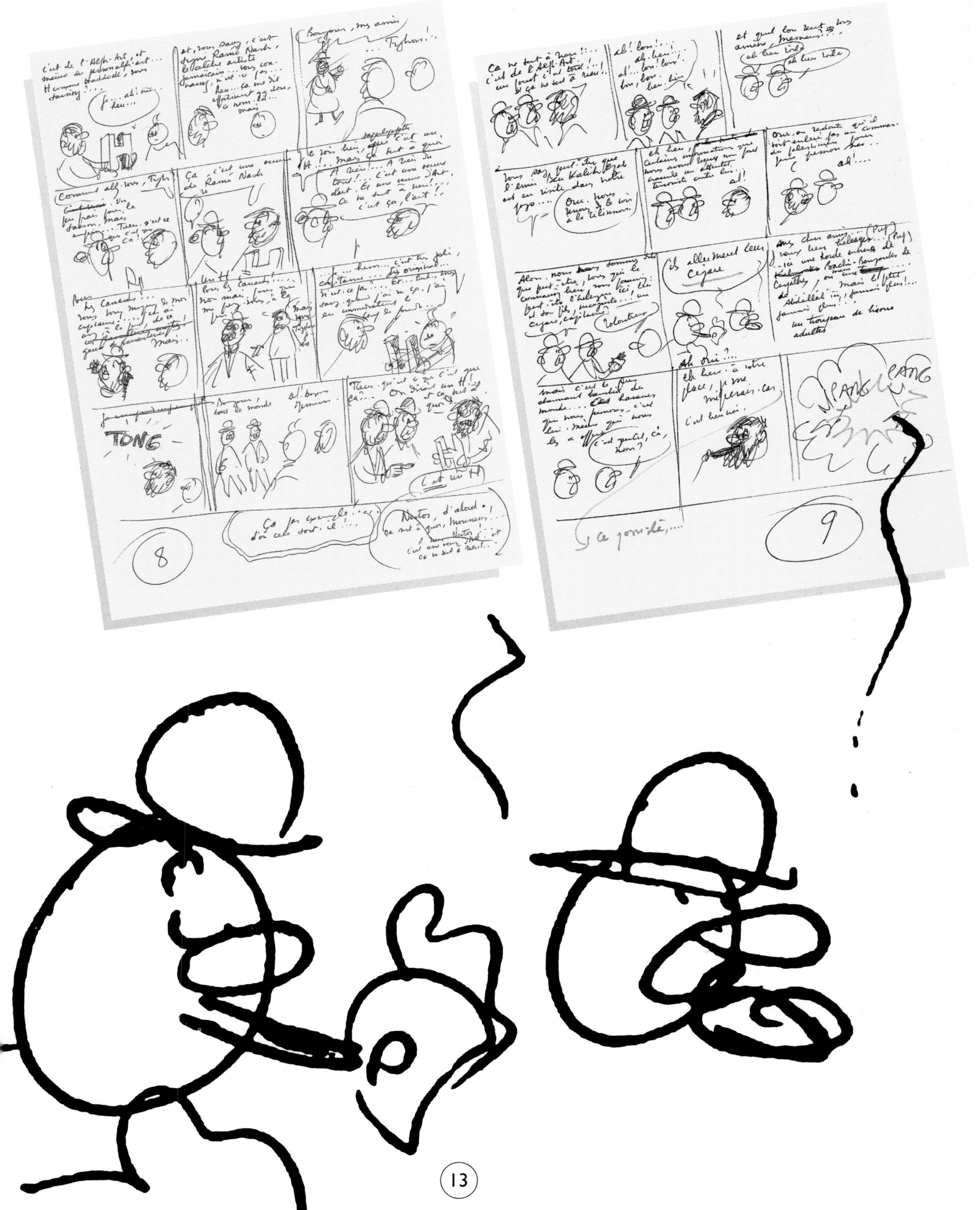
TONG
Volontiers
8
9

HADDOCK *(laughing)*: What did I tell you? Ha, ha! I know that little fiend.

A third BANG; the Captain's cigar explodes.

HADDOCK: Abdullah, just you wait till I catch you…

Jolyon Wagg comes on the scene.

JOLYON WAGG: 'Ello 'ello! What've we got here, then? A war?

THOMSON: Exploding cigars… Someone played a joke on us…

WAGG: Aha, exploding cigars! They were a speciality of my Uncle Anatole. Them and the dribbling glass… *(He sees the sculpture by Ramó Nash)* My, my, what's that thingummy? Looks like an H, eh?

HADDOCK *(crossly)*: Yes, it's an H.

WAGG *(laughing)*: So what's that whatsit for, then?

HADDOCK *(very crossly)*: It is a work of art. It is Alph-Art. It is by Ramó Nash and it is for absolutely nothing at all.

Exit Wagg, highly offended. The telephone rings.

HADDOCK: Hello? No, this is *not* Mr Cutts the butcher… I… What? Ah, I beg your pardon. Just a moment and I'll pass you over to him… *(He hands the telephone to Tintin)* It's the Mr Fourcart I was telling you about…

TINTIN: Hello, yes… Yes, I'm Tintin… Gladly… Tomorrow, late afternoon… Certainly, about six o'clock… Fine!… Till tomorrow then, Mr Fourcart. *(He replaces the receiver and turns to the Captain)* We're really up to our necks in art!... You meet Ramó Nash. You buy some Alph-Art. An expert disappears off Ajaccio. Another expert has something to tell me. Ben Kalish Ezab wants to build an art museum…

Nestor respectfully insinuates himself into the conversation.

NESTOR: Ahem… I…

HADDOCK: Yes?

NESTOR: Will you be needing me again, sir?

HADDOCK: No, Nestor, thank you… *(But, changing his mind, he shows Nestor his new acquisition)* Tell me, Nestor, what do you think of this?... Honestly, now.

NESTOR: What is it, sir?

HADDOCK: It's an H, Nestor, as you can see.

NESTOR: Yes, sir, I do see. And what is it for, sir?

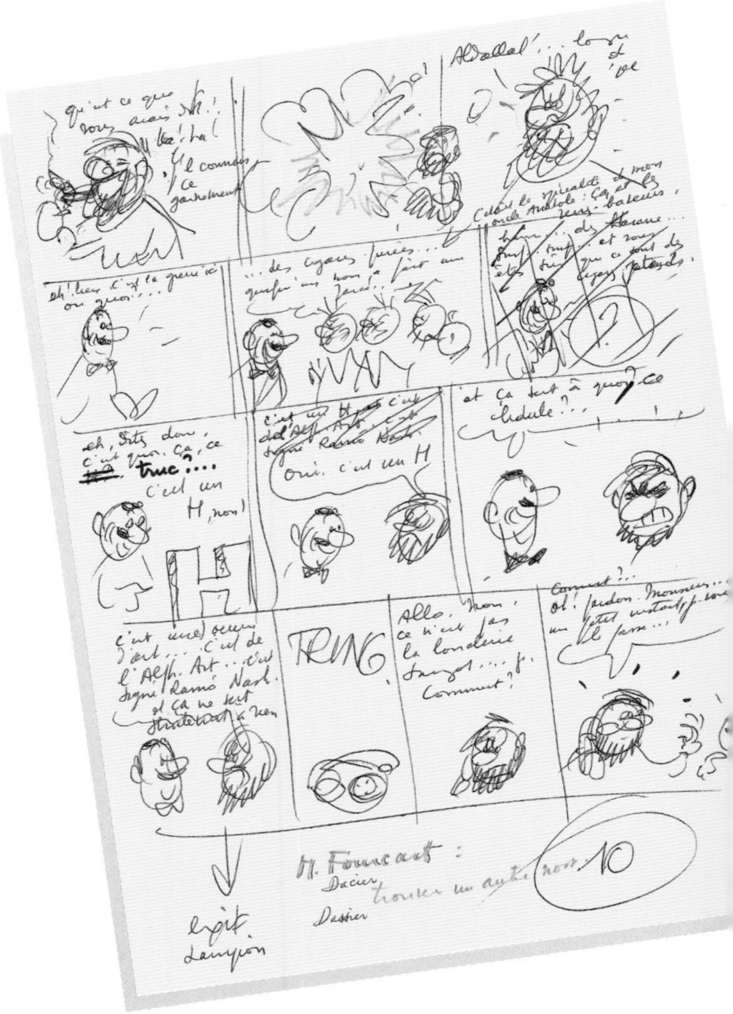
TRING
10

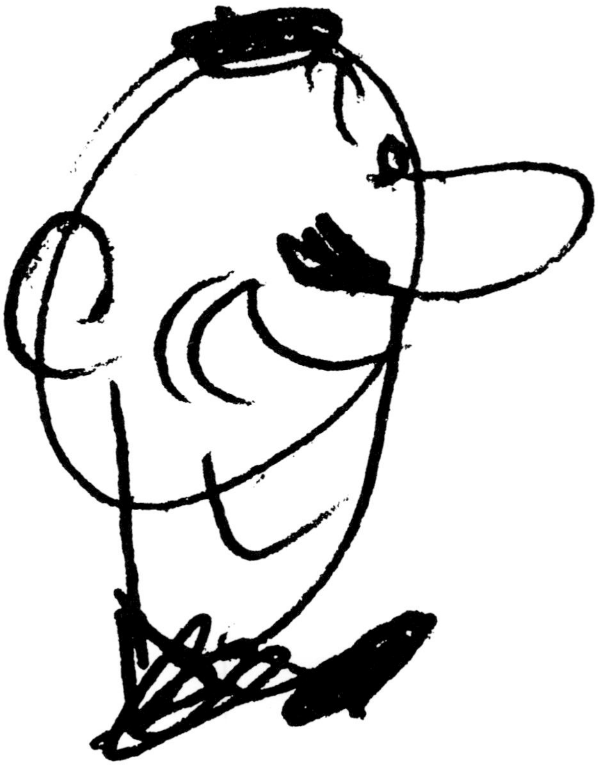

HADDOCK *(furiously)***:** Nothing, Nestor!... Nothing at all! It's a work of art, Nestor… That's obvious, isn't it? And it isn't *for* anything.

THE NEXT EVENING

TINTIN *(Comfortably settled in the drawing room, looks at his watch)***:** Ten to six… Mr Fourcart should be here soon…

But time passes and Mr Fourcart does not arrive.

TINTIN: Half past seven… Our Mr Fourcart surely won't come now… Funny… Has he forgotten our meeting?

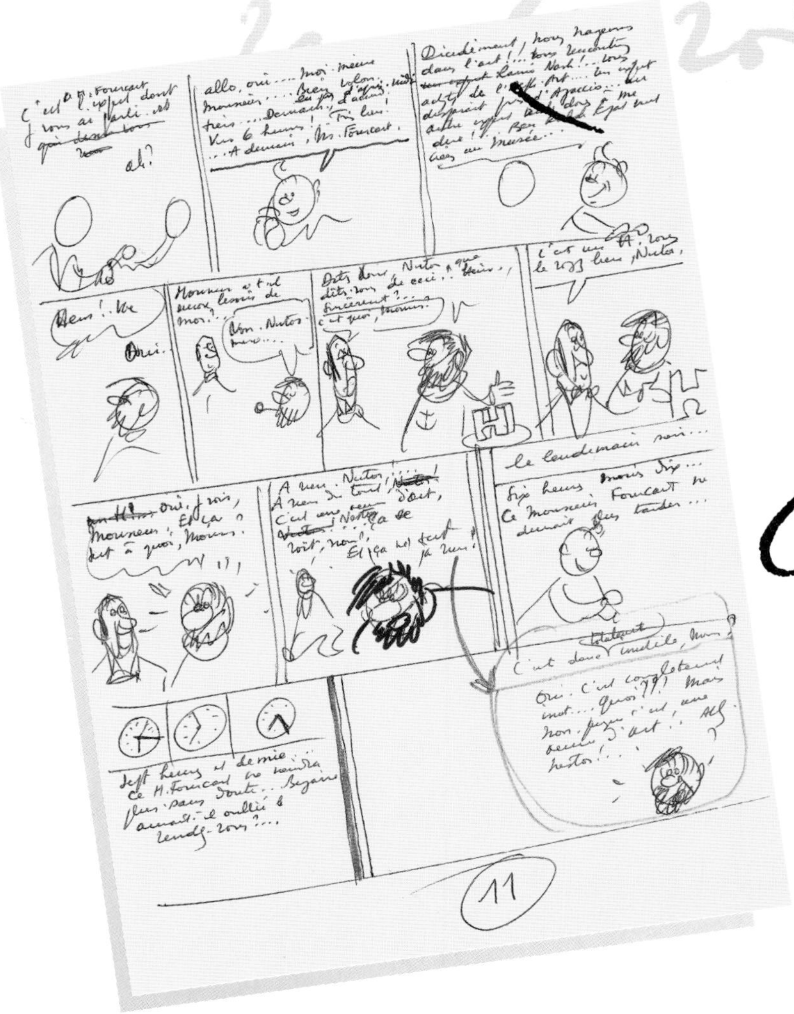

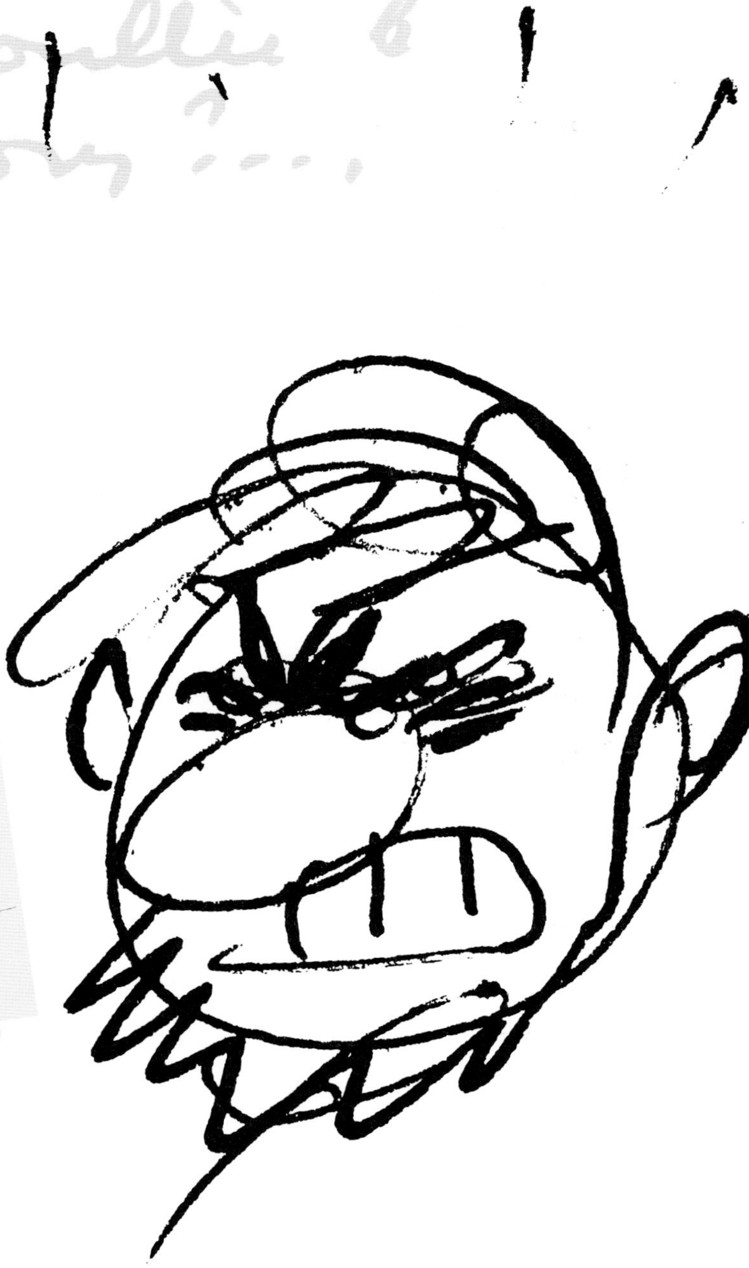

The next morning...

Tintin and the Captain are having breakfast. Snowy arrives, the newspaper in his mouth.

TINTIN: What fresh disaster have they got for us today? *(He opens the paper, reads a few lines, and…)* No! Mr Fourcart is dead!...

HADDOCK: No!

Tintin shows him the article displayed on the front page.

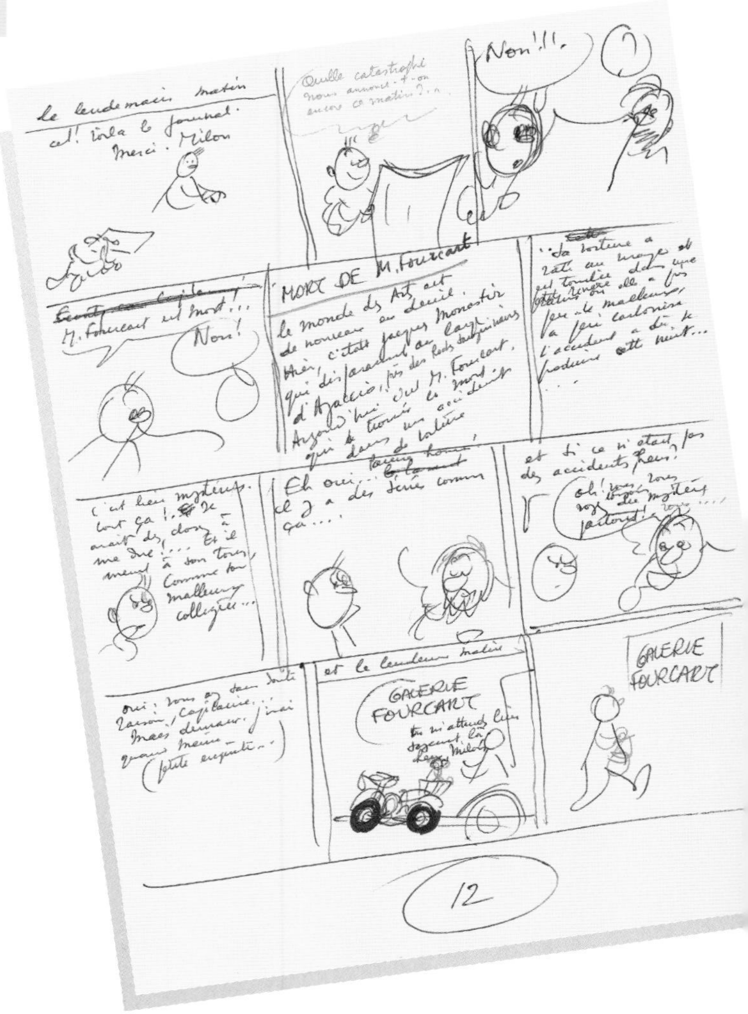
Non!!!
MORT DE M. FOURCART
GALERIE FOURCART
GALERIE FOURCART
12

FOURCART DIES

Art world mourns again

Yesterday, Jacques Monastir disappeared off Ajaccio, near the Sanguinaires islands. Today, the renowned expert Henri Fourcart met his end in an accident. His car skidded on a bend, plunged into a dry riverbed and burst into flames. The doomed driver perished in the blaze.

TINTIN: All very mysterious!... He had something to tell me! And he died, too, like his unhappy colleague.

HADDOCK: Alas yes, poor man! A chapter of accidents…

TINTIN: But what if they weren't accidents, eh?

HADDOCK: Oh, you! You always see mysteries everywhere!

TINTIN: Yes, you're probably right, Captain… But even so, tomorrow I shall make a few enquiries.

THE NEXT MORNING

Tintin parks his motor scooter outside the Fourcart gallery.

TINTIN: You wait there quietly for me, Snowy my friend.

Tintin is met by the assistant with the large spectacles.

THE ASSISTANT: Good morning, sir. Can I help you?

TINTIN: I… er… Well, it's like this… My name is Tintin. I'm a journalist. Mr Fourcart telephoned me two days ago. He said he had something important to tell me. He said I would have all the essentials for a sensational article. We made a date, and just before his visit he had his accident.

THE ASSISTANT: Alas yes, sir.

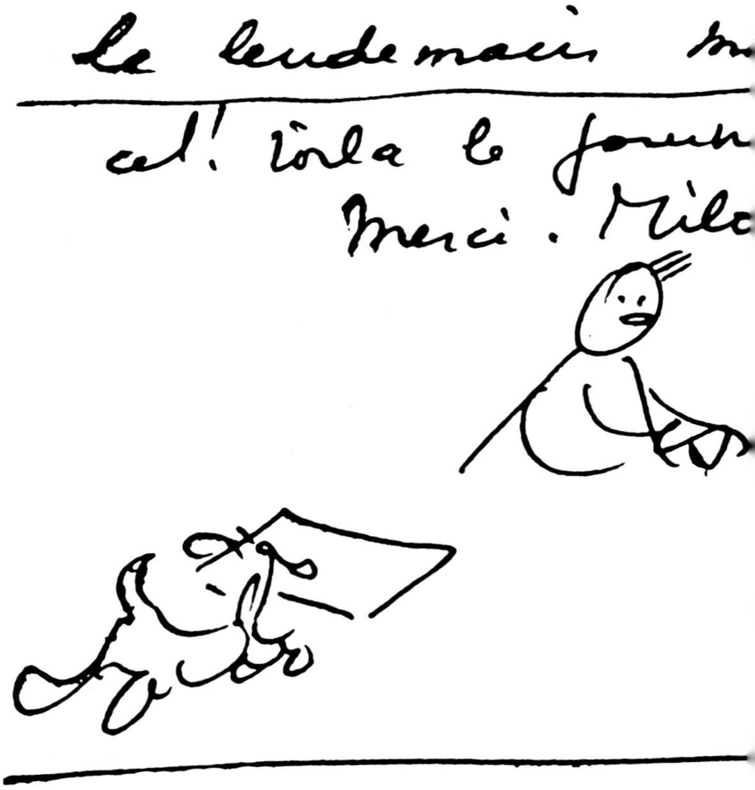

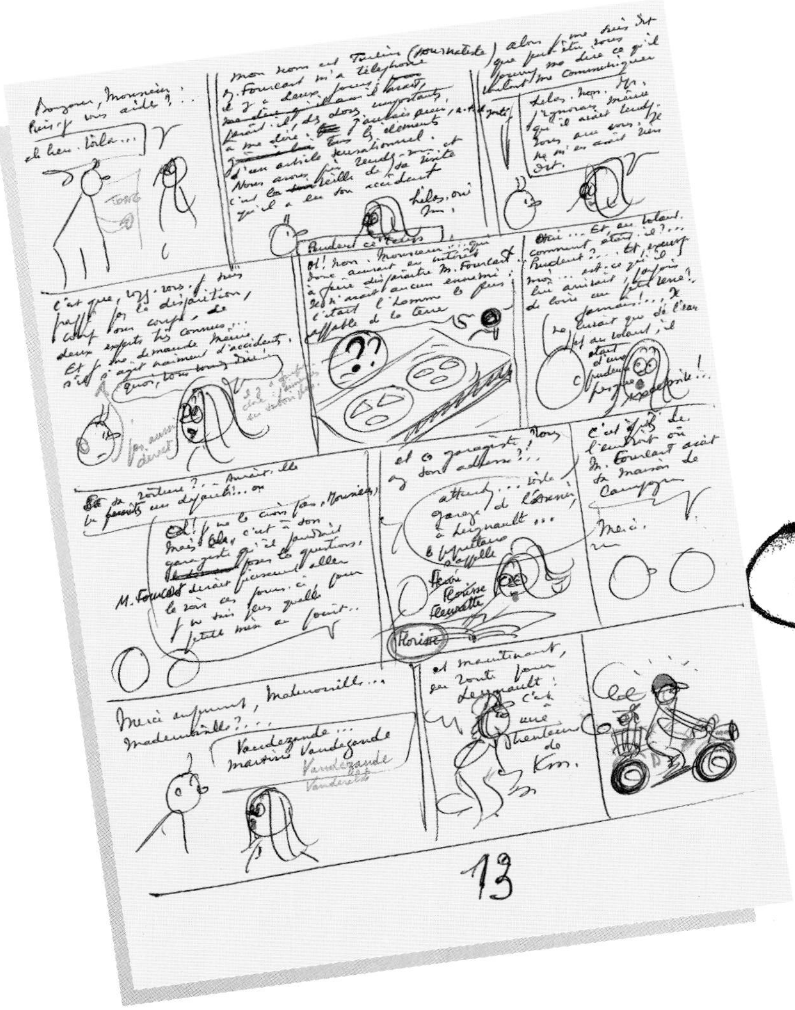

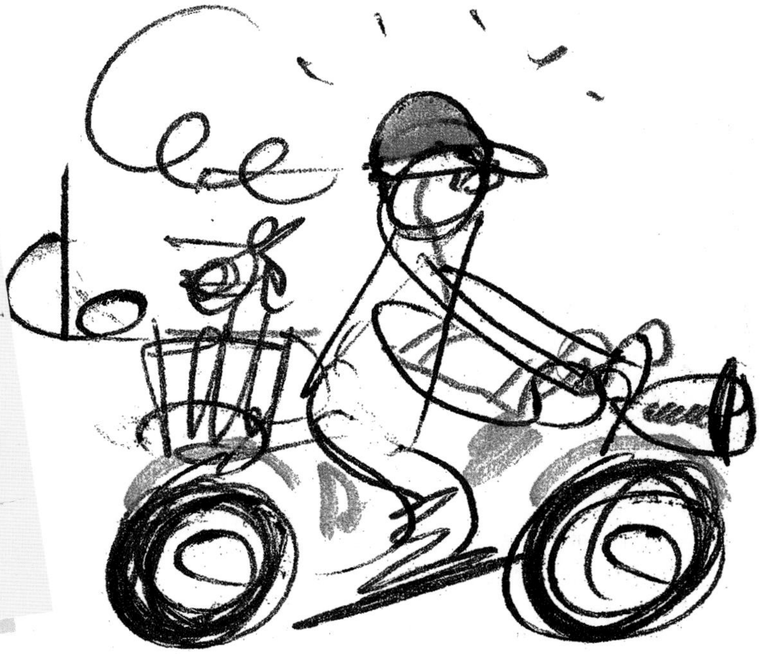

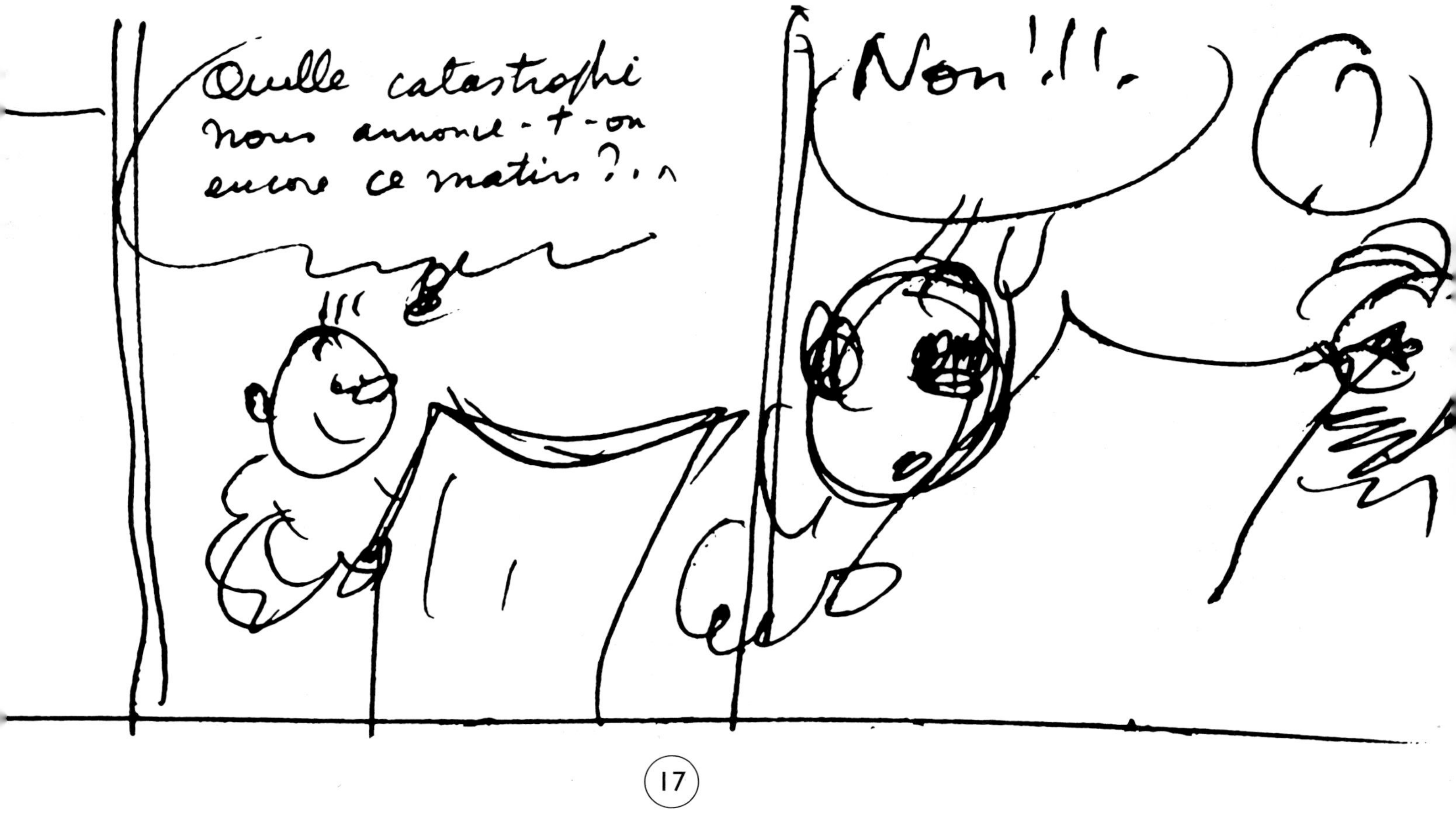

Quelle catastrophi nous annonce-t-on encore ce matin?..
Non!!!

Tintin investigates...

TINTIN: I was wondering whether perhaps you knew what he wanted to tell me...

THE ASSISTANT: Alas no, sir. I didn't even know he had a meeting with you. He said nothing about it.

TINTIN: You see, it's just that I was struck by the disappearance, one after another, of two very well-known art experts. And I even began to wonder if they really were accidents.

THE ASSISTANT: What? You mean...

Hidden beneath the counter, a recorder is taping the conversation.

THE ASSISTANT: Oh, sir... Who could have wanted to get rid of Mr Fourcart? He hadn't a single enemy. He was the nicest man in the world.

TINTIN: Yes... And what was he like as a driver?... Careful?... Forgive me, but did he sometimes have a glass or two?

THE ASSISTANT: Never! He drank only water. As for driving, he was almost too careful.

TINTIN: And his car? Could it have had something wrong with it... Or...

THE ASSISTANT: Oh, I don't know. That's a question for his garage. Mr Fourcart had just been to see them in the last few days, for some little job or other...

TINTIN: This garage: have you got the address?

THE ASSISTANT: Wait... *(She consults a card)* There, the Garage de l'Avenir at Leignault. The owner is called Fleurotte. It's near the place where Mr Fourcart had his country house.

TINTIN: Thank you very much, Miss... Miss?...

THE ASSISTANT: Vandezande... Martine Vandezande.

Outside, Tintin finds Snowy waiting patiently on the back of the scooter.

TINTIN: Now, off to Leignault: it's thirty kilometres.

At Leignault, Tintin stops in front of the Garage de l'Avenir. He sees a mechanic with a moustache.

TINTIN: Mr Fleurotte?

FLEUROTTE: That's me, yes.

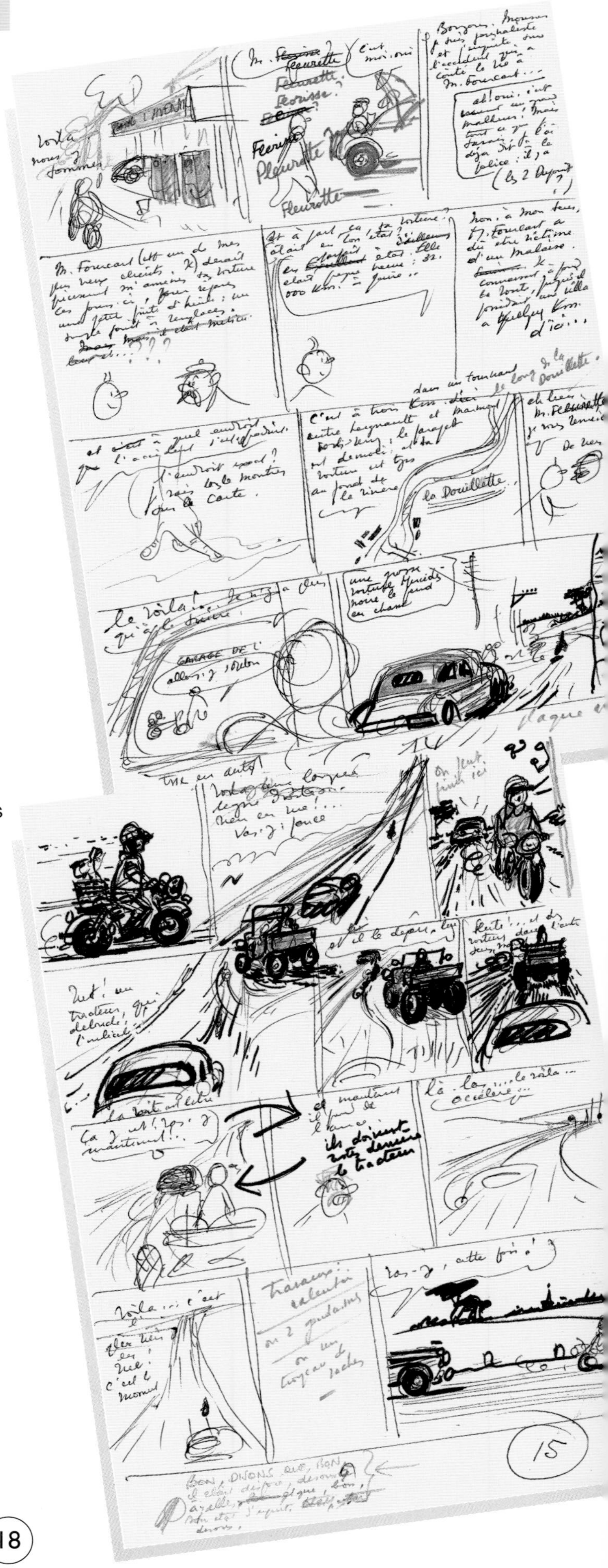

la Douillette
15

TINTIN: Good morning. I'm a journalist, and I'm making some enquiries about the accident in which Mr Fourcart was killed.

FLEUROTTE: Oh, yes. What a tragedy. But I've already told the police everything I know. Mr Fourcart was one of my oldest customers. He actually brought in his car just a few days ago to have a small oil leak attended to: just a seal replacement job.

TINTIN: And apart from that, the car was in good shape?

FLEUROTTE: Perfect condition. It was almost new: less than 32,000 kilometres on the clock. No, to my way of thinking, Mr Fourcart must have been taken ill. He knew the road well. He had a house not far from here.

TINTIN: Whereabouts did the accident happen?

FLEUROTTE: The exact place? I'll show you on the map. It's three kilometres from here, between Leignault and Marmont. You'll see, the parapet is smashed and the car is still on the bed of the river, the Douillette.

TINTIN: Thank you very much, Mr Fleurotte.

FLEUROTTE: That's OK.

TINTIN: Let's go, Snowy.

Tintin remounts his scooter and drives away. A powerful black Mercedes follows him.

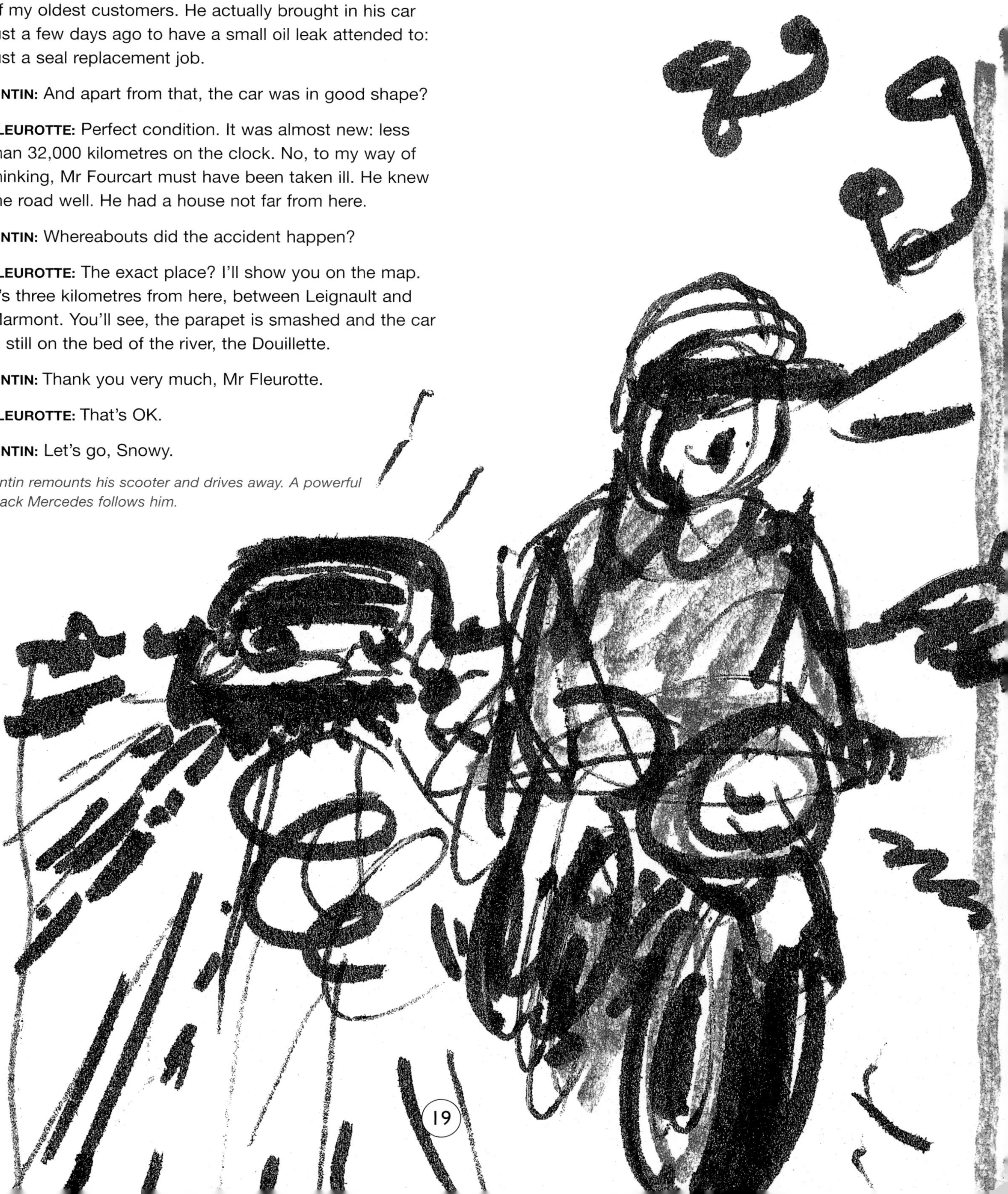

The pursuit...

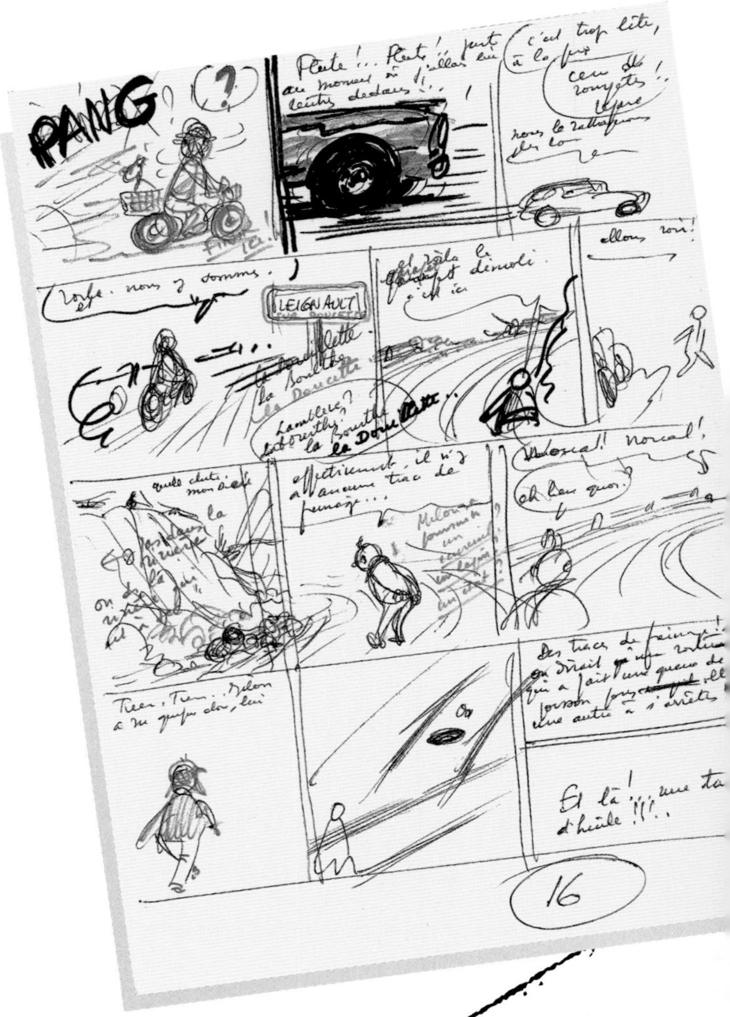
PANG
LEIGNAULT
16

ONE OF THE PURSUERS: A long straight bit. Nothing about!... Go on, put your foot down!... Look at that! A jeep pulling out! The idiot!... And he's passed it on his scooter… Hell's teeth! And now there are cars coming the other way… He's getting ahead.

After following the jeep for some distance, the Mercedes finally manages to pass.

ONE OF THE PURSUERS: That's it!... Now go! There, that's him… step on it! Nothing in sight… now's our chance!

But the occupants of the Mercedes are out of luck. On the brow of the hill two policemen are watching the traffic. After this new setback, the Mercedes at last closes up on Tintin. Now it is only a few metres behind.

ONE OF THE PURSUERS: This time, get him!

Suddenly, a loud bang makes Tintin and Snowy look round. The Mercedes has blown a tyre.

THE DRIVER: Blast!... Blast!... Just when I was going to hit him! What a farce!

While the occupants of the Mercedes change the wheel, Tintin reaches the scene of the accident.

TINTIN: Ah, here we are. There's the broken parapet. This is the place. *(He stops, parks his scooter against a low wall, crosses the road and approaches the ravine)* Let's see. Crumbs! What a drop! *(Leaning over, he sees down below the burnt-out wreckage of the car; then he examines the roadway)* No sign of skid marks, anyway…

Meanwhile, Snowy starts to chase a rabbit, but after a short distance he stops and starts to bark furiously.

TINTIN: Hello… Snowy's found something. Skid marks. Looks as if a car cut in front of another to make it stop!... And there… A pool of oil! *(He stands in the road, thinking)* Let's see, the garage man talked about a *small* oil leak… But perhaps the car was standing for quite a long time… And if someone forced Fourcart to stop… then it really was murder… And the other 'accident', to Monastir, was murder as well!

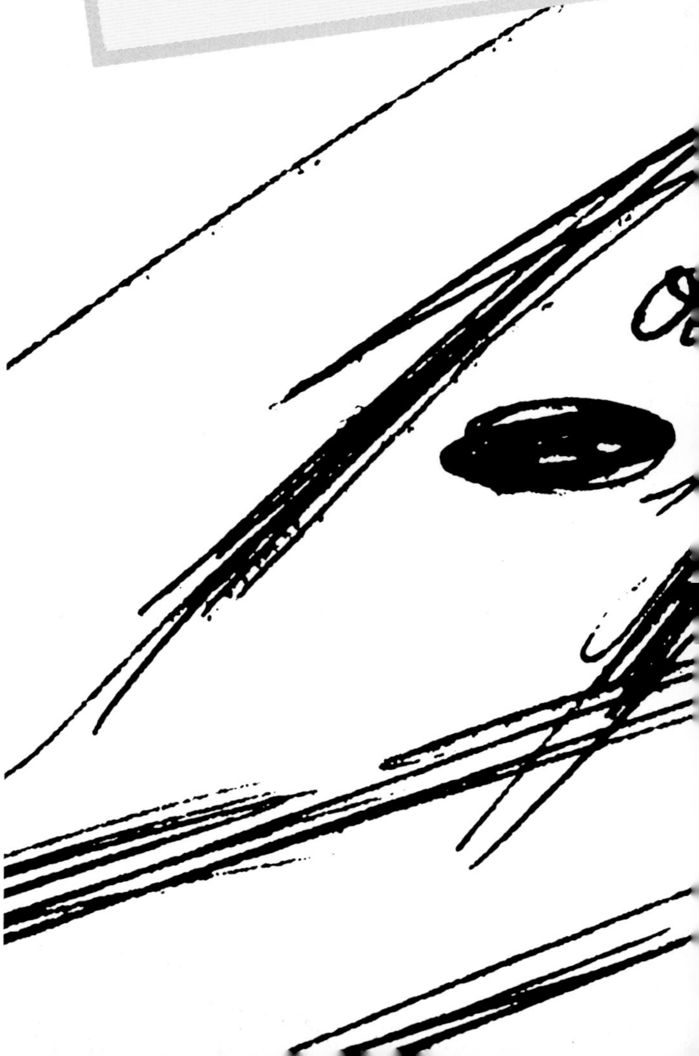

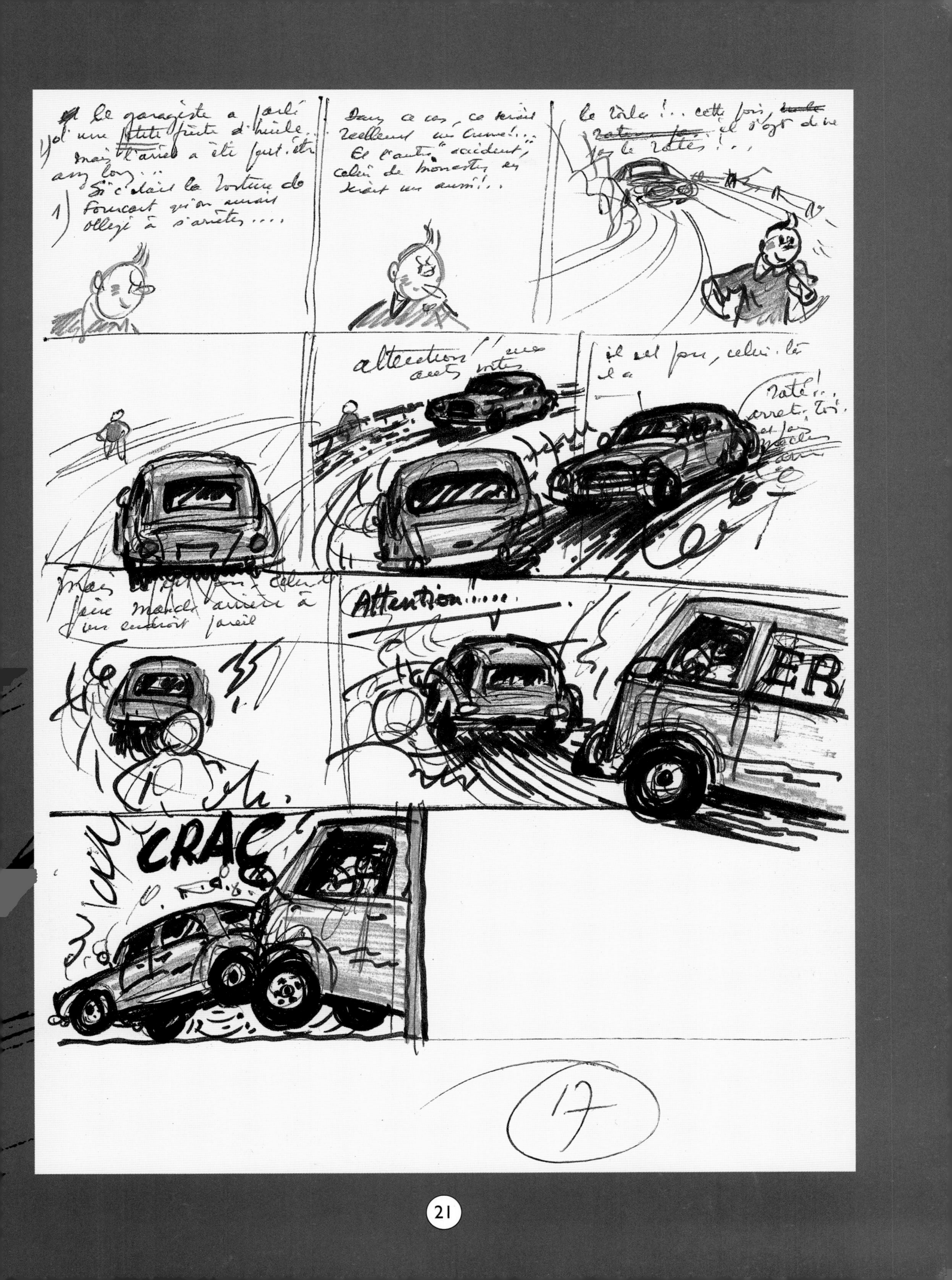

Attention !....
ER
CRAC
17

Deep in thought, Tintin doesn't notice the Mercedes approaching at full speed.

ONE OF THE PURSUERS: There he is!... This time, don't miss!...

The Mercedes starts to swerve to hit Tintin, but another car suddenly comes from the other direction.

ONE OF THE PURSUERS: Look out! A car!

DRIVER OF THE OTHER CAR: He must be crazy!

ONE OF THE PURSUERS: Missed! Stop here and reverse back…

Tintin watches the manoeuvre.

TINTIN: That's dangerous! Reversing in a place like this!... Look out!

Too late! The Mercedes is rammed by a van coming from behind.

ONE OF THE PURSUERS: Get going! Get going! We've botched it!

The Mercedes disappears in a cloud of dust.

THE VAN DRIVER *(getting out)*: Those people must be absolutely daft… *(He notices a sub-machine-gun on the ground and stoops to pick it up)* I say, look at this!

TINTIN: Don't touch it!... There'll probably be fingerprints. *(He carefully picks up the gun with a handkerchief)* I'm taking this to the police. But first of all, I'm going after them.

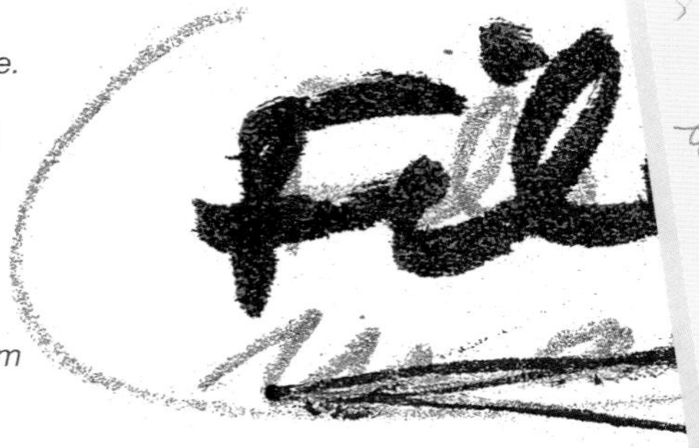

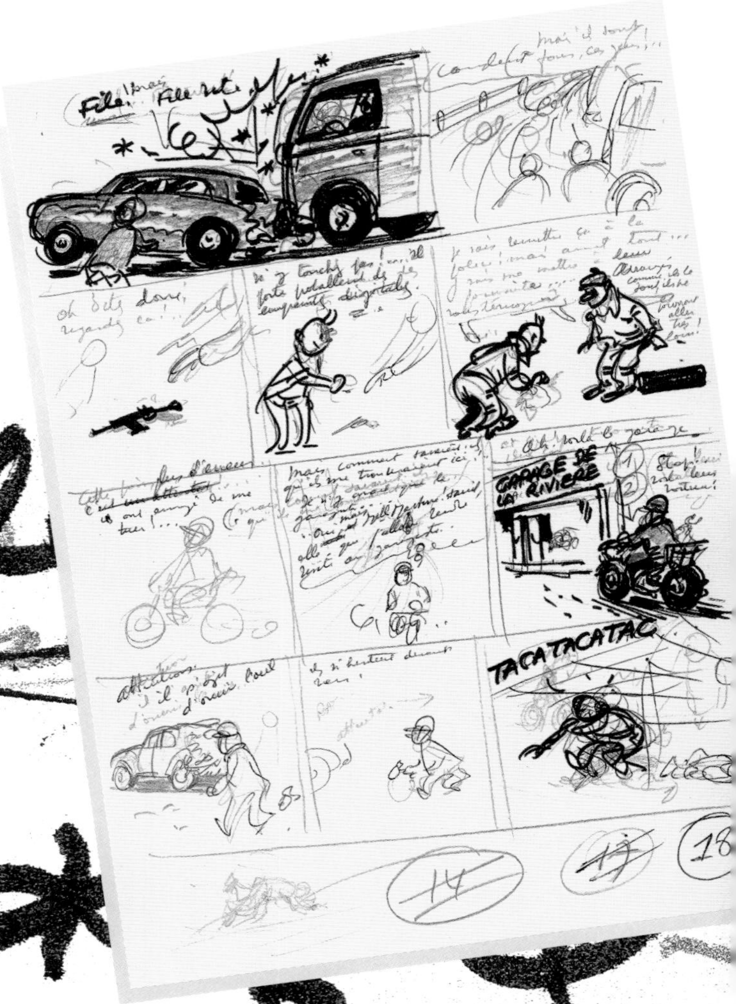
GARAGE DE LA RIVIERE
TACATACATAC

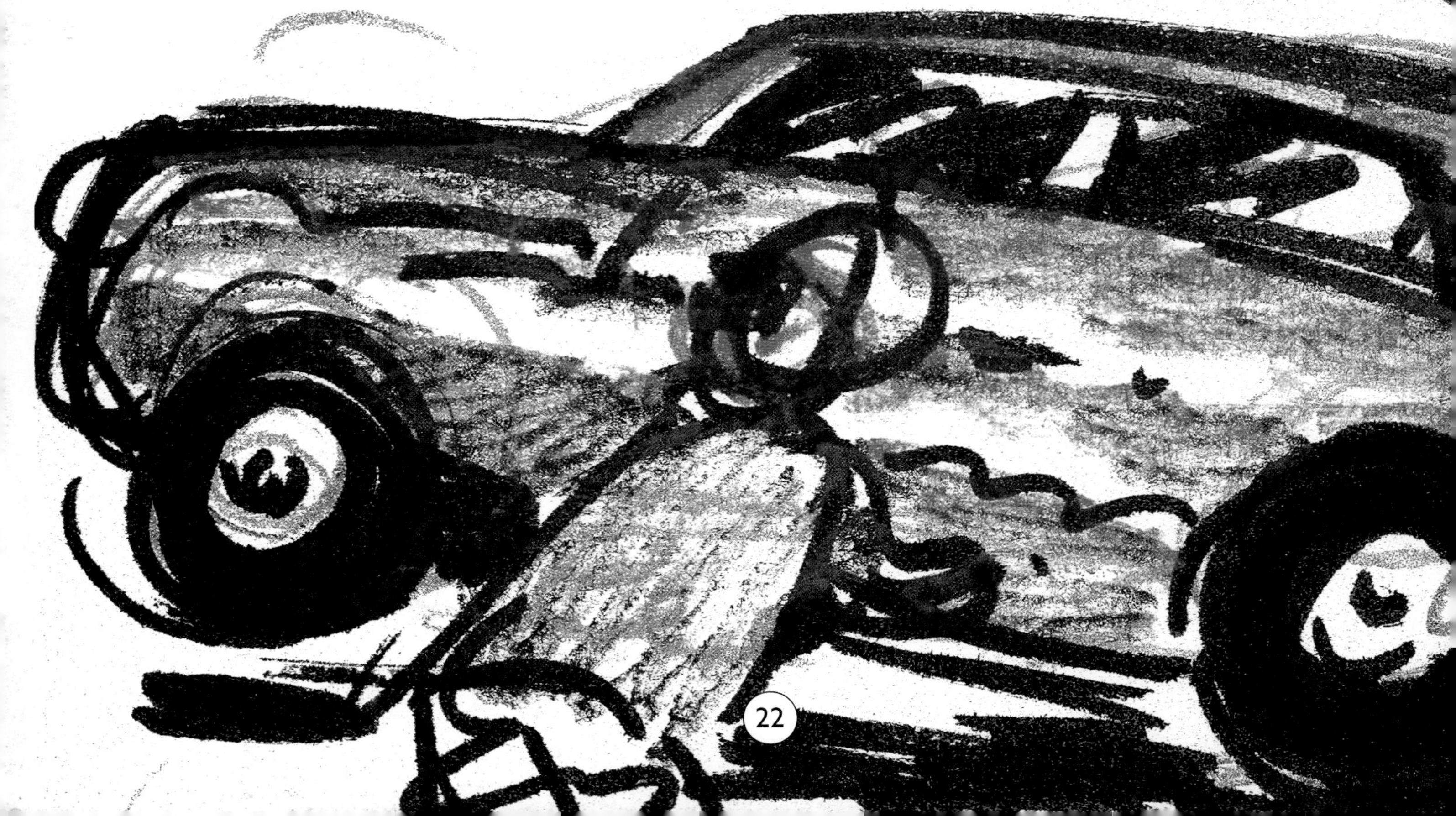

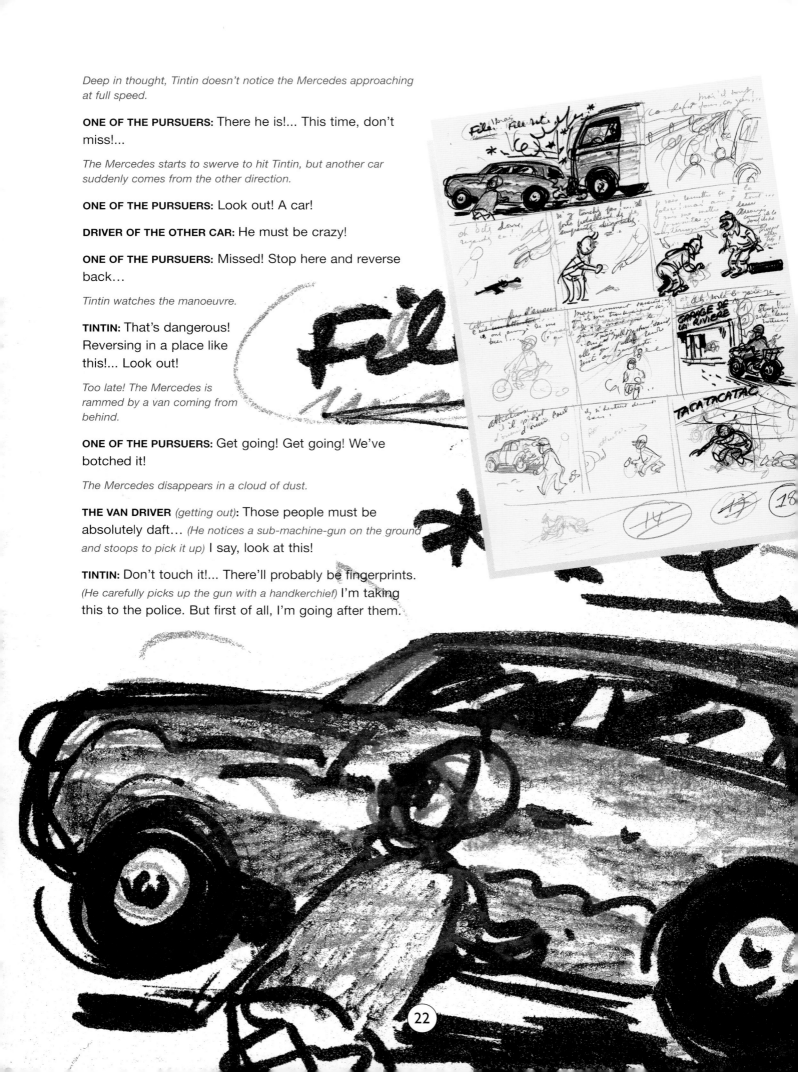

THE VAN DRIVER: In the state they're in, they won't get far.

TINTIN *(driving away on his scooter)***:** This time there's no mistake. They tried to kill me. But how did they know they'd find me here? Only the garage-man… Yes, but Miss Martine, she knew I was going to see the garage-man… Stop! There's their car!

The Mercedes has pulled up outside a garage. Tintin hides behind a damaged 2CV.

TINTIN: Careful! I must keep my eyes open. They'll stop at nothing.

At that very moment there is a series of loud explosions. Tintin hurls himself to the ground.

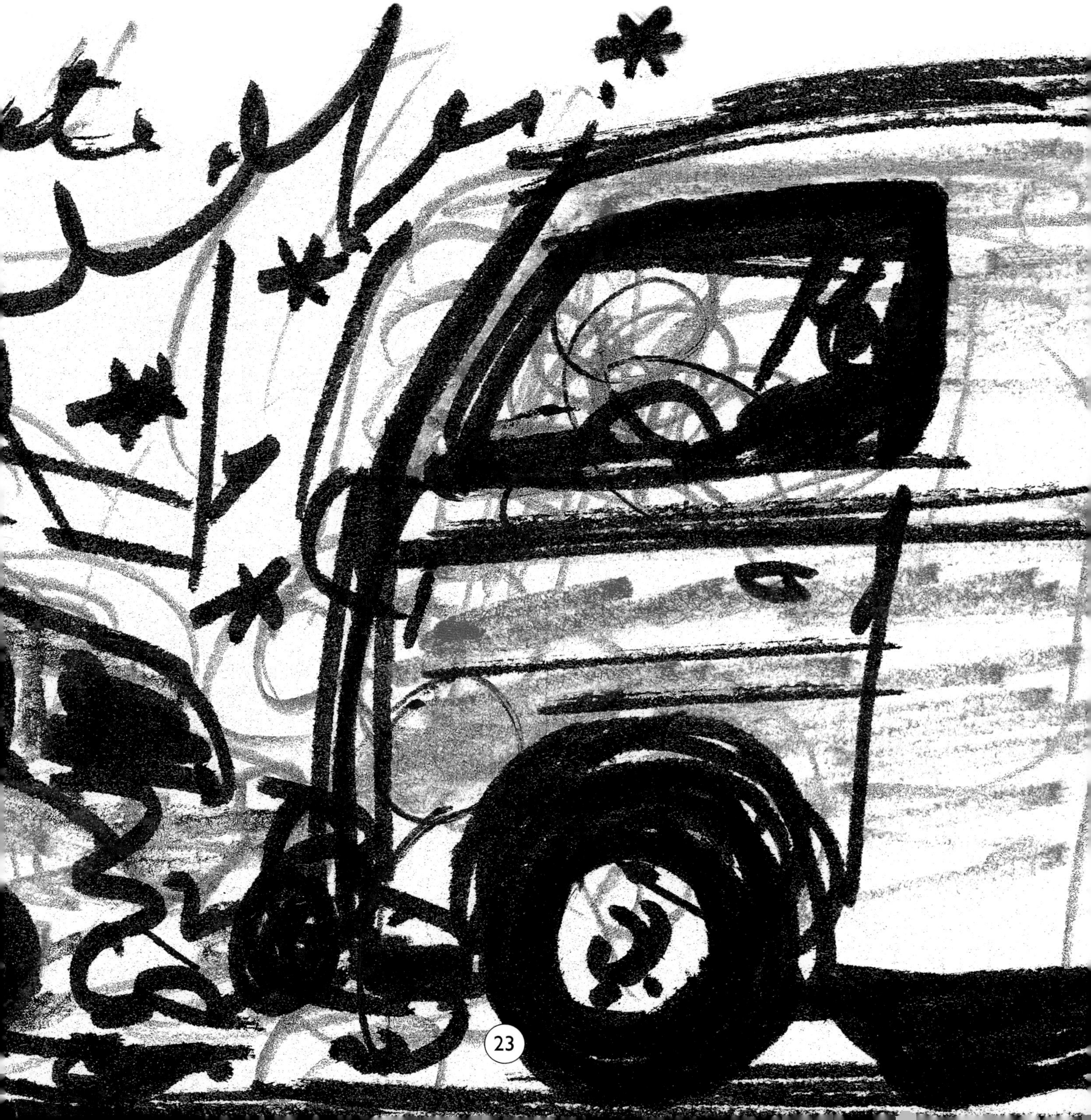

Return to the gallery...

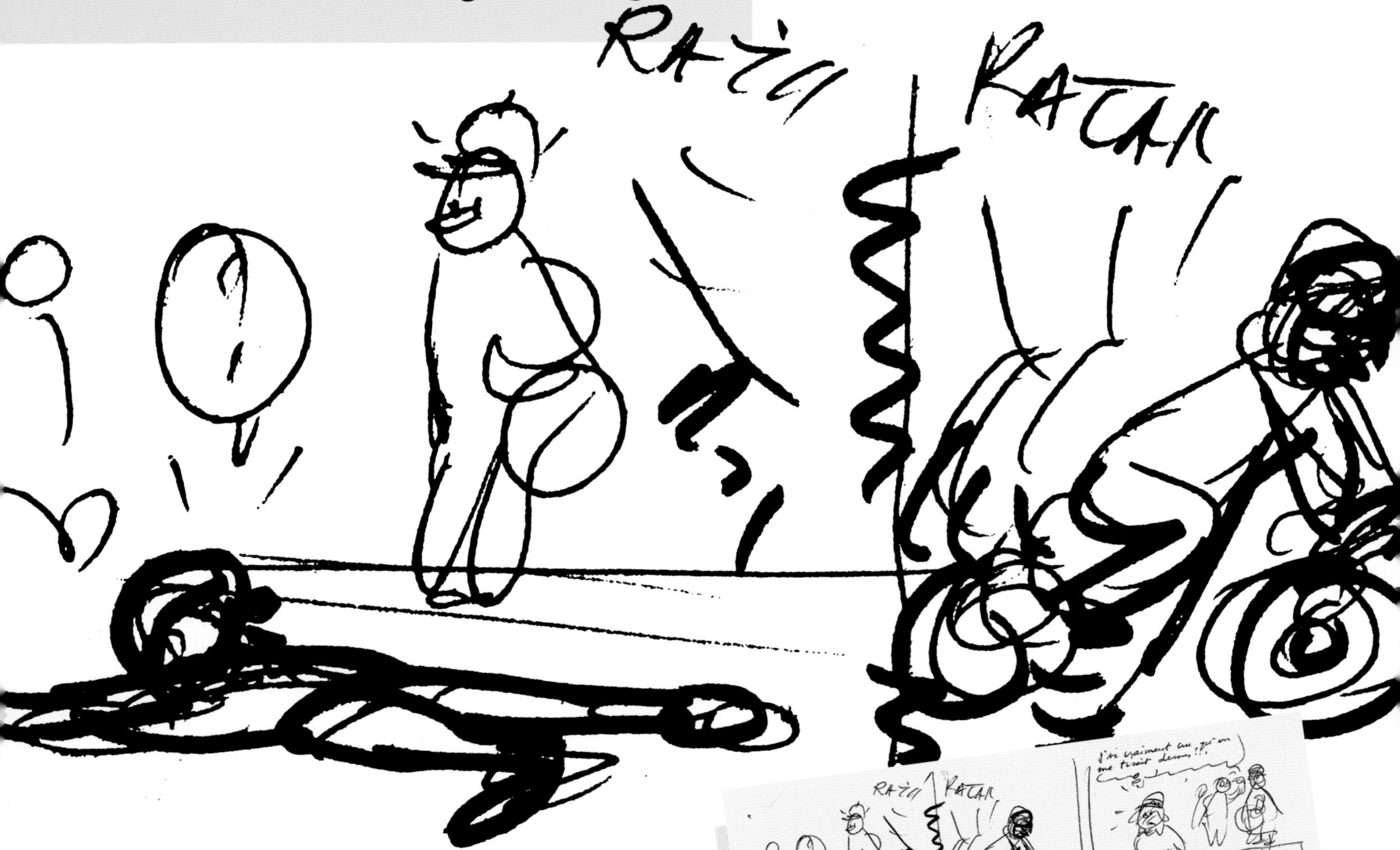

It was only a noisy motorcycle starting up. A mechanic watches Tintin with amazement.

TINTIN: I really thought someone was shooting at us!!!

SNOWY: We looked pretty silly, you know...

TINTIN *(to a group of mechanics who are arguing fiercely)*: Excuse me, but d'you know where the people from that Mercedes have gone?

THE FOREMAN: That's just what we'd like to know ourselves! They arrived here and stole a car belonging to that gentleman there, while he was filling up. We're waiting for the police... Are you looking for them too?

TINTIN: I'll say so! They tried to kill me... Ah, here come the police!

HALF AN HOUR LATER

TINTIN *(Setting off again on his scooter)*: You keep a lookout behind us, Snowy! If you see anything unusual, bark... Now, off to Marlinspike. It won't be easy to explain all this to the Captain.

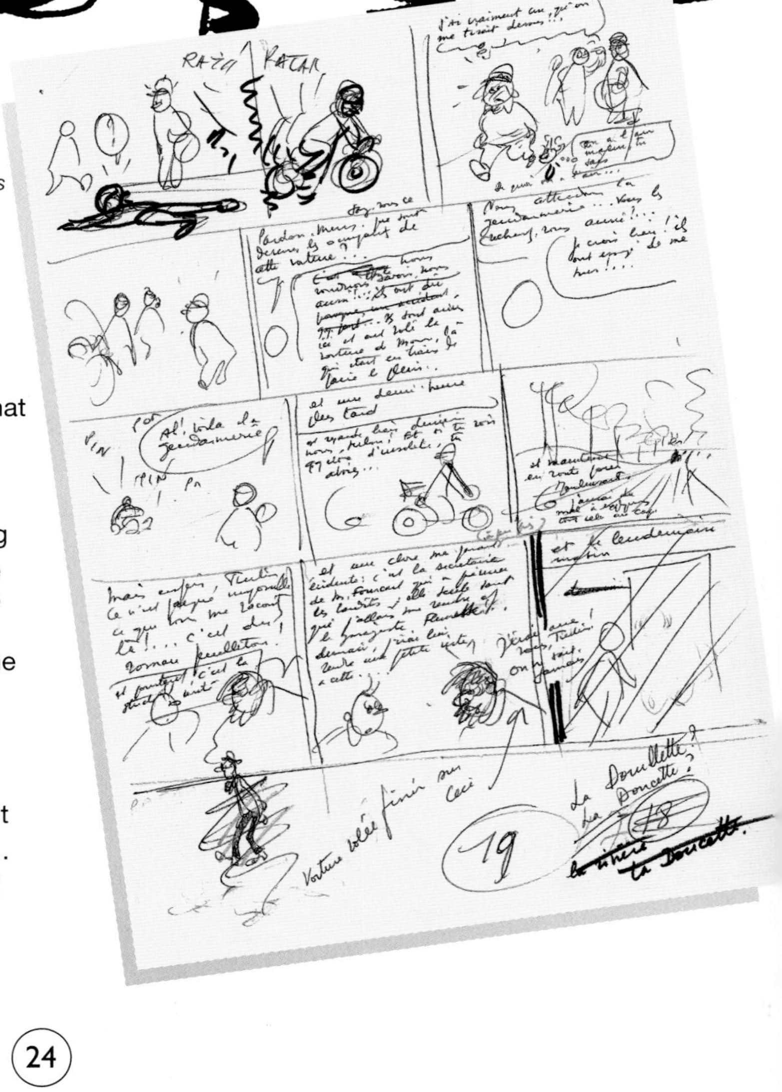

Captain Haddock reacts as Tintin had foreseen.

HADDOCK: Honestly, Tintin! What you're telling me can't be true!… It's like a cheap thriller…

TINTIN: Nevertheless, it is absolute fact. And one thing seems fairly obvious to me: Fourcart's assistant tipped off the gangsters. She was the only one who knew I was going to see Fleurotte at the garage. Tomorrow I shall be paying a visit to that young lady.

HADDOCK: I'll go with you, Tintin. You never know.

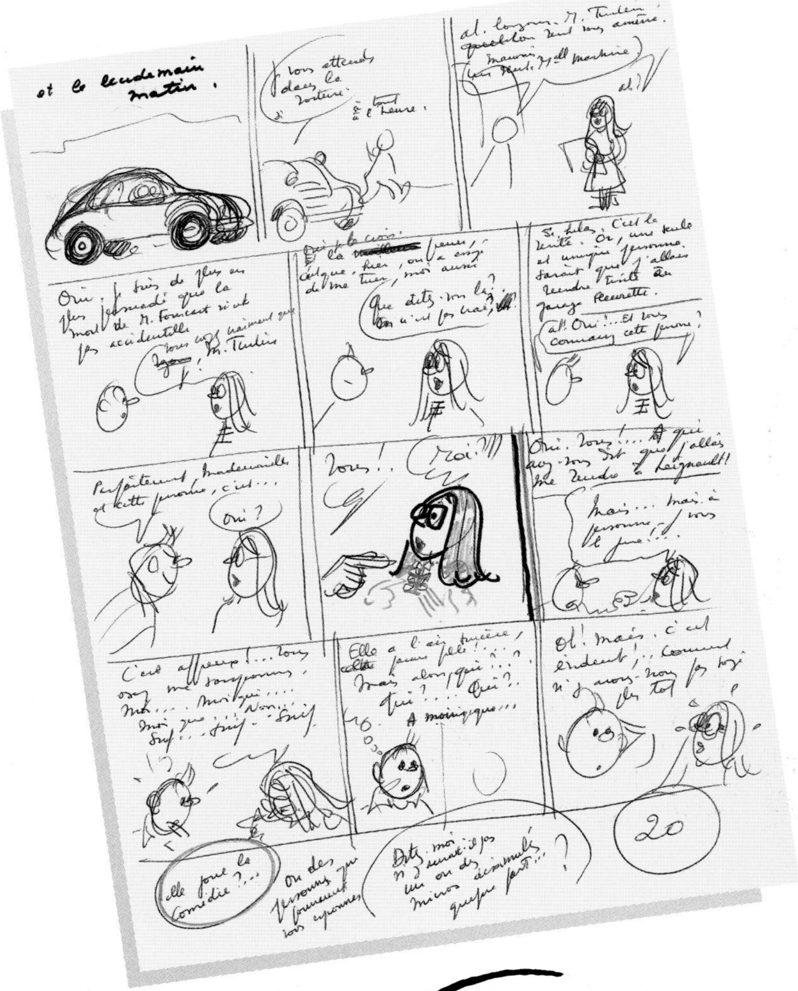

20

THE NEXT MORNING

HADDOCK *(Stopping his car outside the Fourcart Gallery)*: I'll wait for you in the car…

THE ASSISTANT: Ah, good morning, Mr Tintin. To what do we owe the pleasure?

TINTIN: Not so much a pleasure, Miss Martine.

THE ASSISTANT: Oh?

TINTIN: Yes, I am more and more convinced that Mr Fourcart's death was not an accident.

THE ASSISTANT: Mr Tintin, you really believe…?

TINTIN: Yes, I do. And the proof is that yesterday someone tried to kill me too.

THE ASSISTANT: What did you say? It can't be true!

TINTIN: Alas, yes… only too true. Now, one single person knew that I was going to see Fleurotte at the garage.

THE ASSISTANT: Oh, yes… And you know who that person is?

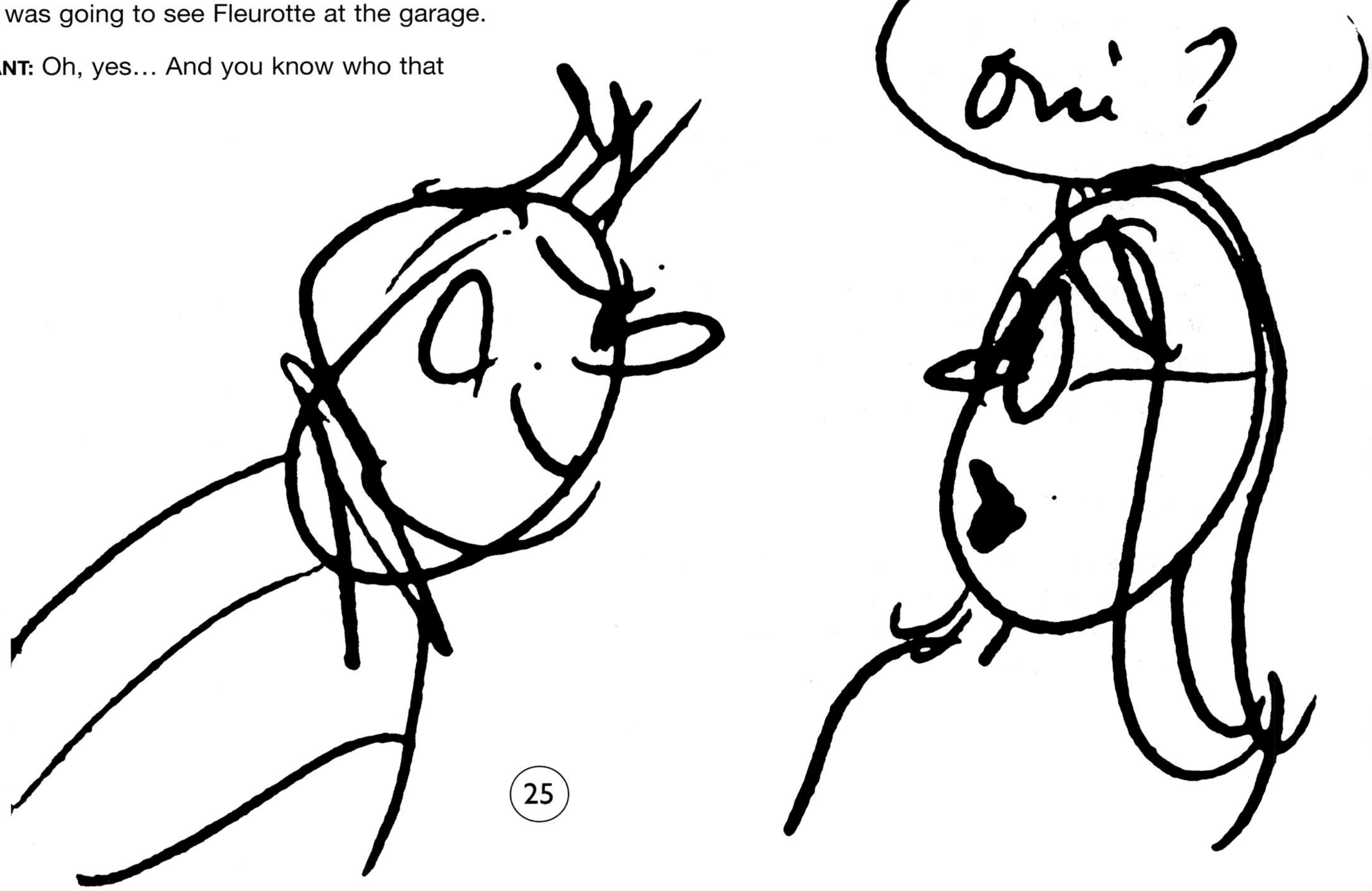

Oui ?

TINTIN: Absolutely, Miss Vandezande… and that person is…

THE ASSISTANT: Yes?

TINTIN: You!

THE ASSISTANT: Me?

TINTIN: Yes, you!... Who did you tell I was going to Leignault?

THE ASSISTANT: But… I told no one, I swear to you!... *(She bursts into tears)* It's dreadful!... You dare to suspect me… Me who… Me who… No!... Sniff… sniff… sniff…

TINTIN *(thoughtfully)***:** She seems to be sincere, this girl… But who, then?... Who?... Who?... Unless… Oh, it's obvious, why didn't we think of it before?... Tell me, is there anyone else besides you here in the gallery?

THE ASSISTANT: Oh, yes… That office belongs to Mrs Laijot, the book-keeper.

TINTIN: Is she here all the time?

THE ASSISTANT: No, she only comes in once a fortnight…

TINTIN: In that case it couldn't be her. *(He goes into the next room)* Mrs Laijot?

MRS LAIJOT: Yes, that's me. Twenty-five years I've worked here like a slave… I've worn out my eyesight in the service of this company. And after that to be suspected of I don't know what…

TINTIN *(Goes back to reception)***:** It certainly isn't her. She's a shrew, that's a fact, but she's honest.

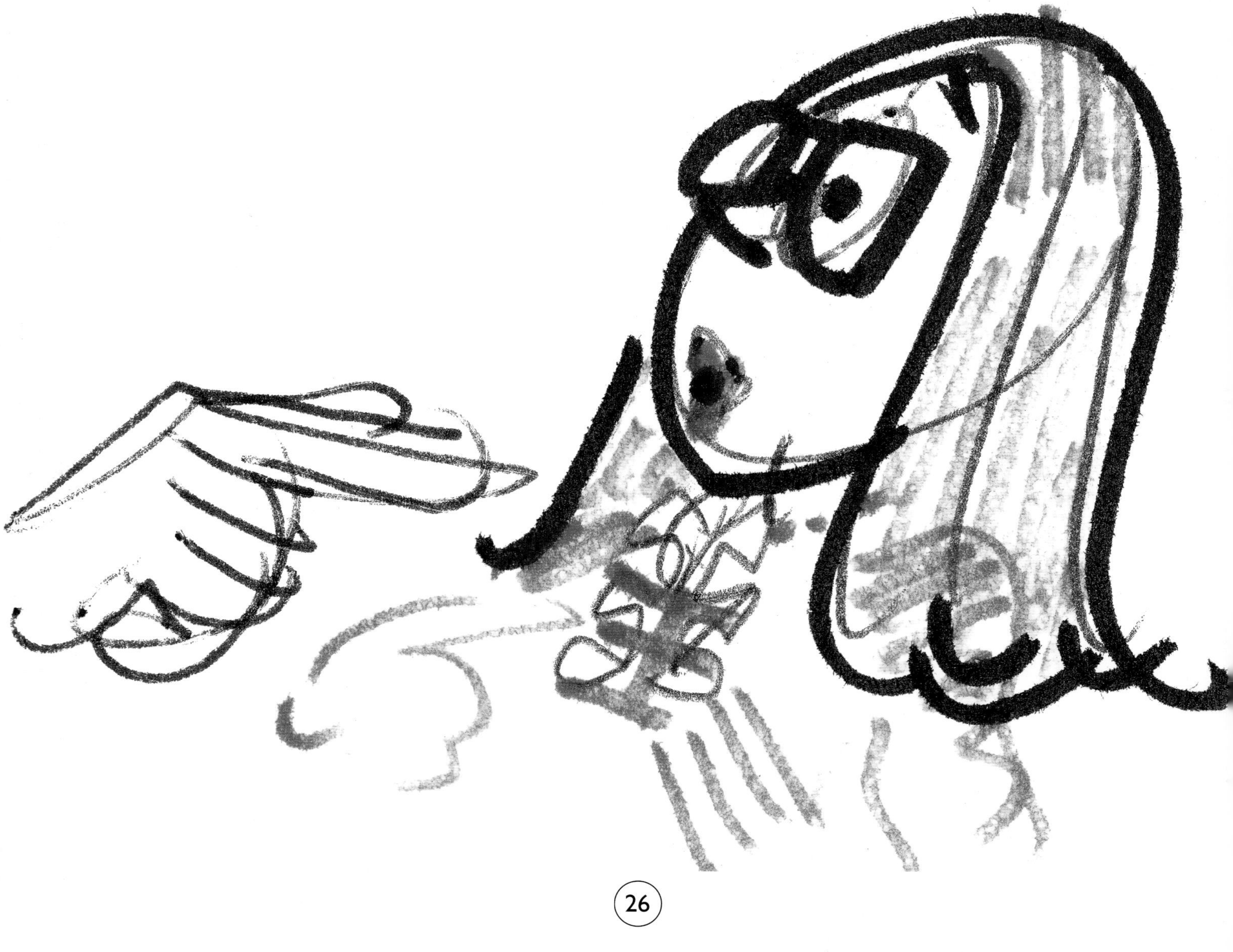

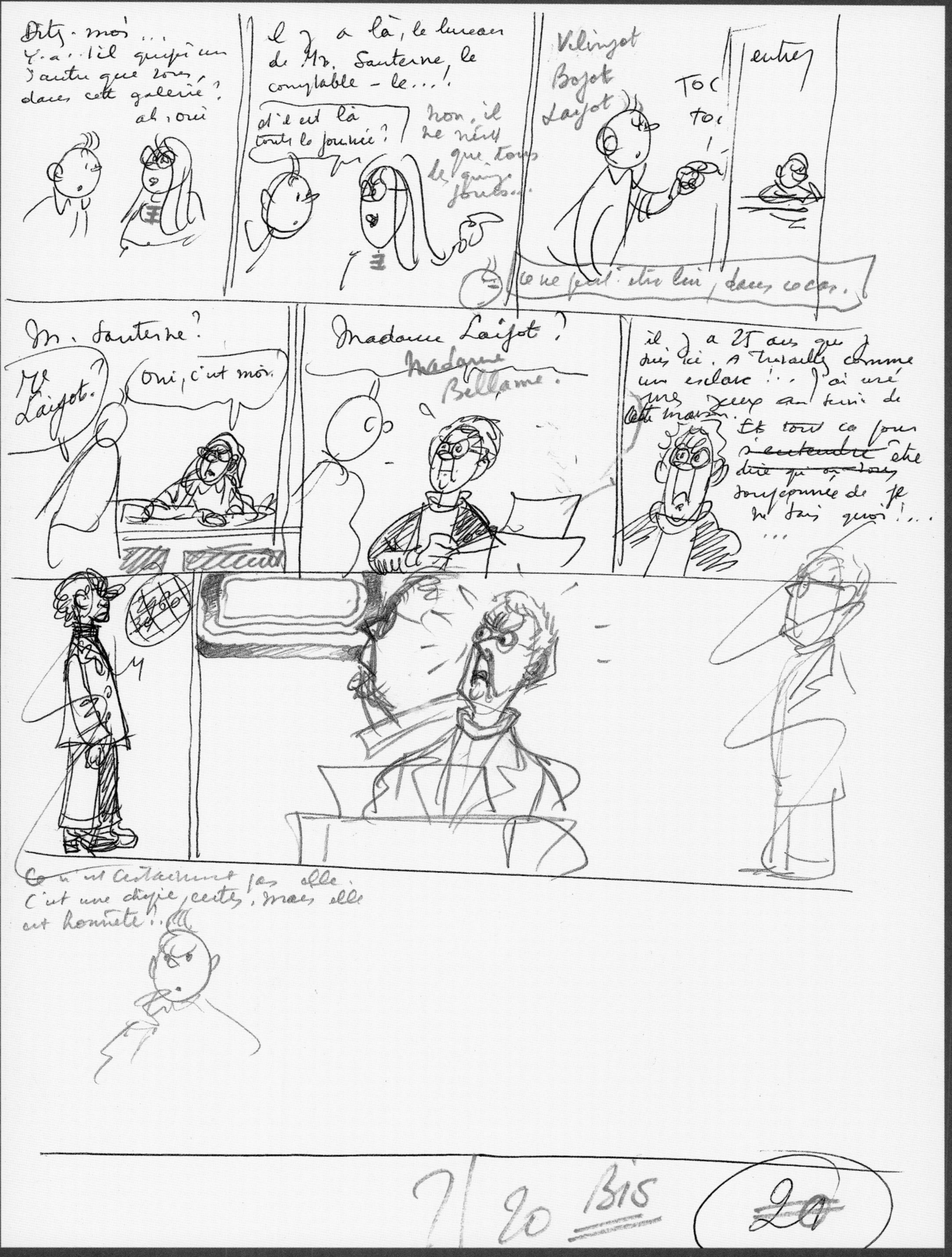

Dites-moi... Y a-t-il quelqu'un d'autre que vous, dans cette galerie?
Ah, oui
Il y a là, le bureau de Mr. Santerne, le comptable - le...!
Il est là toute la journée?
Non, il ne vient que tous les quinze jours...
Vlinzot
Bojot
Laijot
TOC TOC
Ce ne peut être lui, dans ce cas.
entrez
Mr. Santerne?
Me Laijot?
Oui, c'est moi.
Madame Laijot?
Madame Bellamme.
Il y a 25 ans que je suis ici. A travailler comme un esclave!.. J'ai usé mes yeux au service de cette maison. Et tout ça pour être soupçonnée de je ne sais quoi!...
C'est une chipie, certes, mais elle est honnête!
20 BIS
20

Endaddine Akass...

TINTIN *(to the assistant):* There, there! Don't cry any more!... I've thought of something. What if there are microphones hidden somewhere in the office? Bugs which record all conversations?

THE ASSISTANT: But why? Whatever for?

TINTIN: I don't know any more than you, but we'll look all the same...

In the car the Captain is beginning to be impatient.

HADDOCK: Young Sherlock Holmes is taking his time.

AND HALF AN HOUR LATER

HADDOCK: Ah, there he is... Well?...

TINTIN: Nothing!... I don't understand it at all.

HADDOCK: Good. We'll go home.

The car stops at a red light. As the Captain moves off, Tintin sees a huge poster.

TINTIN: Stop, Captain! Stop!

HADDOCK: What? What is it?

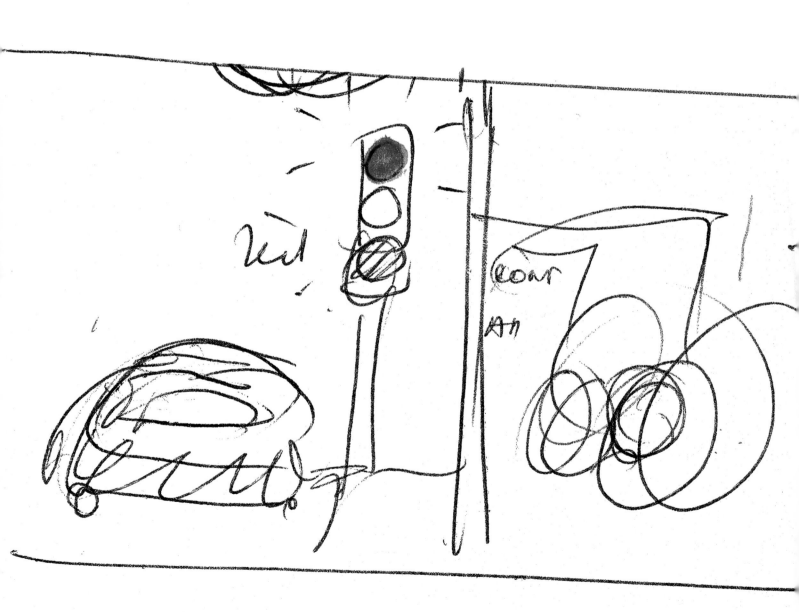

Tintin gets out of the car and goes up to the poster. It depicts an odd-looking man with a beard and a moustache, a small round hat and large spectacles, wearing a curiously shaped pendant. His name stands out in large letters: ENDADDINE AKASS, together with the title of a conference: Health and Magnetism.

TINTIN: That jewel reminds me of something… But what? Or who?... Oh, Miss Martine! She was wearing one like it!... Is she a disciple of this famous mystic, then?... Why don't I go to the meeting?... This must be the Endaddine Castafiore was talking about.

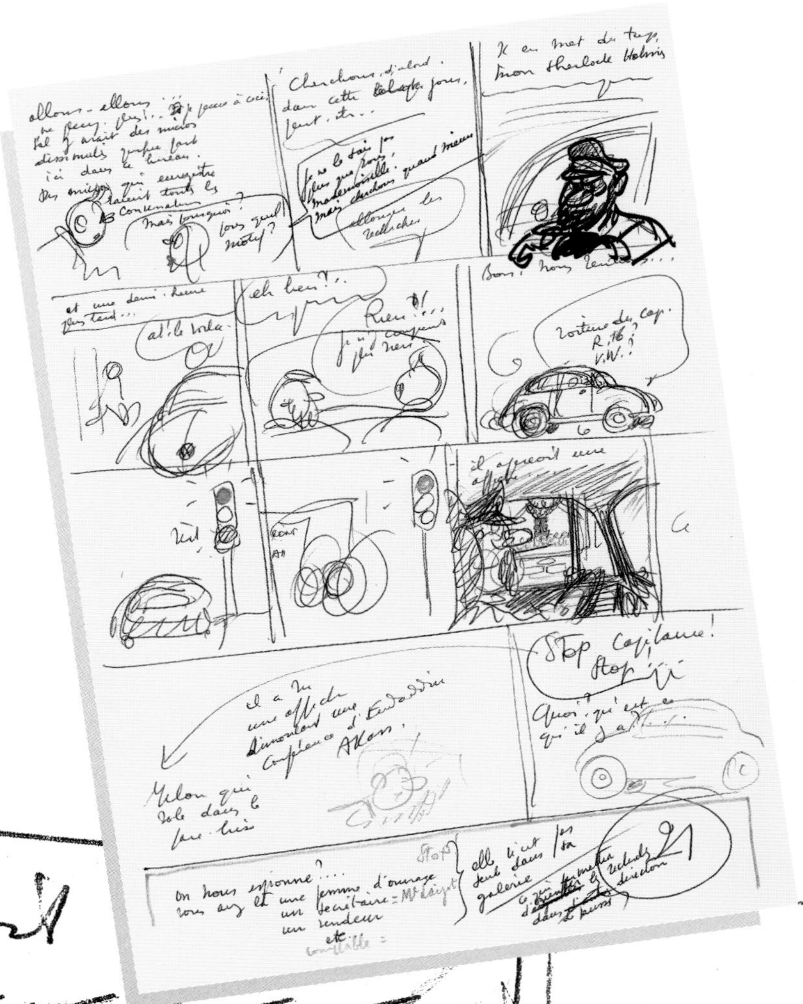

Stop Capitaine! Stop!!

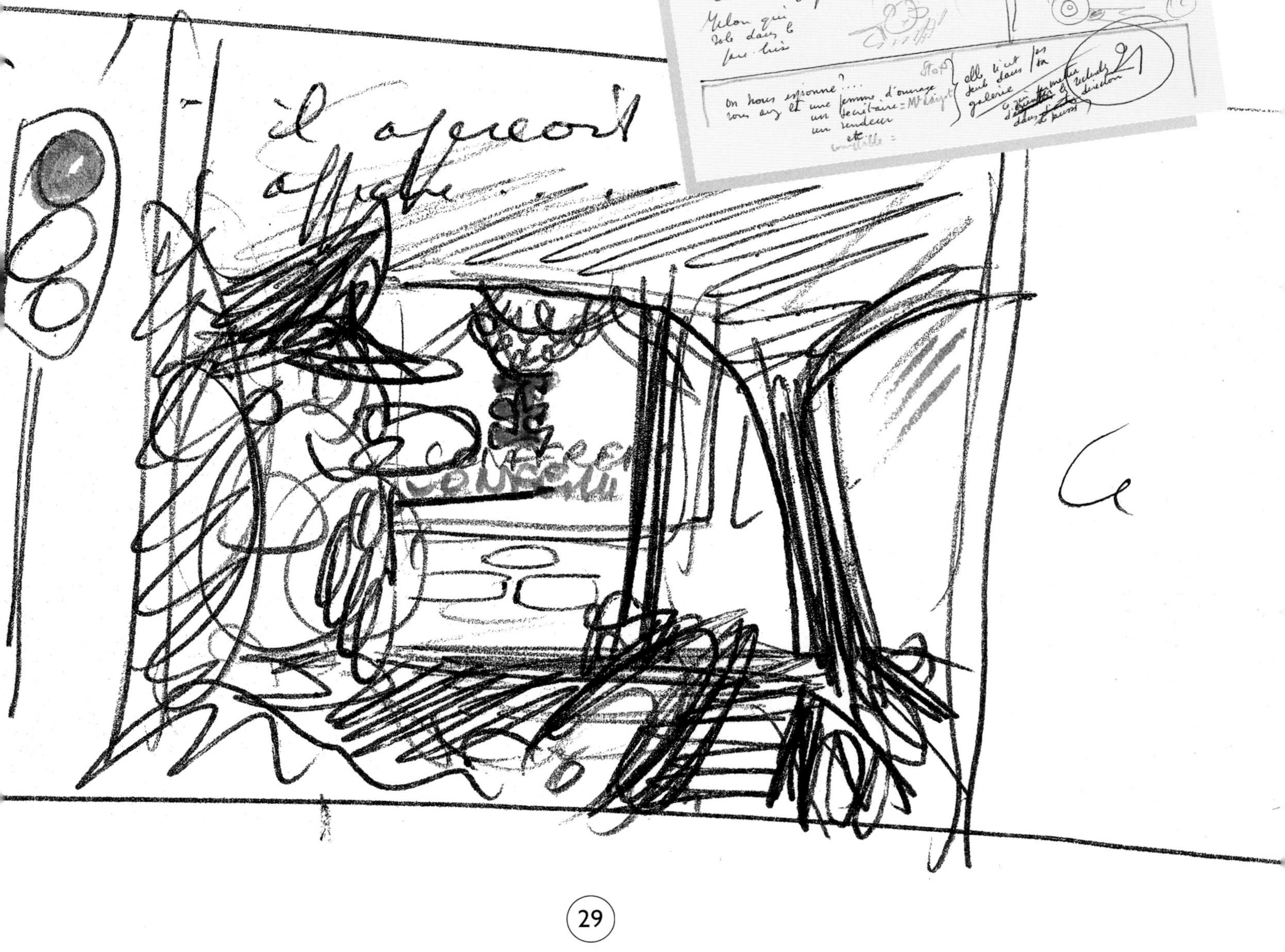

il aperçoit affiche

Health and magnetism...

HADDOCK: If you want to... Let's go!

THAT EVENING

Decorating the speaker's table is the jewel motif noticed by Tintin. A presenter comes forward.

THE PRESENTER: Ladies and gentlemen, it is my privilege to introduce the celebrated mystic Endaddine Akass. May I ask you to rise...

The audience rises, among them Tintin and the Captain. The master makes his entrance, attended by an acolyte. He speaks with a strong accent.

ENDADDINE: I sense a hostile presence, a sceptical spirit which disturbs the atmosphere...

HADDOCK: What's the ectoplasm waiting for?

TINTIN: He's gathering his thoughts, he's concentrating, he's meditating.

VOICES: Ssh! Ssh!

ENDADDINE: My dear brothers, my dear sisters, I'm going to ask you to say together, with me, the sacred syllable, after which your power...

HADDOCK: Don't turn round at once, but to your right... and a little behind you... *(Taking a discreet glance, Tintin sees the Thompsons)* What are those two jellyfish doing here?... That's what I'm wondering...

TINTIN: And there... someone else I know... Look, it's Mr Sakharine.*

The session begins. The master is concentrating. But the Captain has a violent fit of sneezing. He sneezes several times, blows his nose loudly, drops his pipe and hunts for it between the rows of the audience. In short, he completely disrupts the proceedings.

*See *The Secret of the Unicorn*

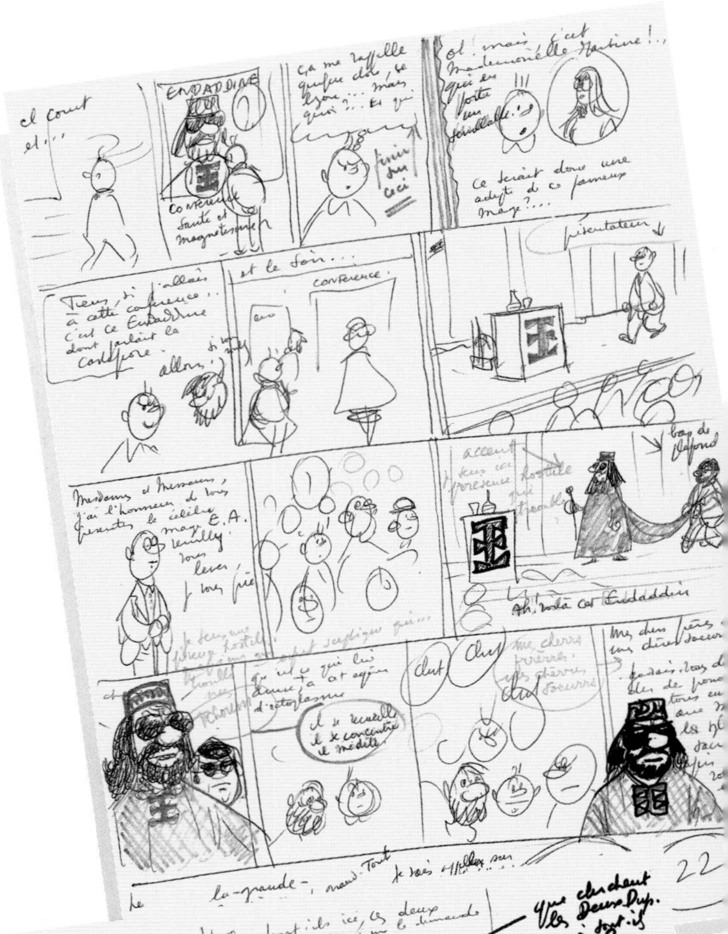
22

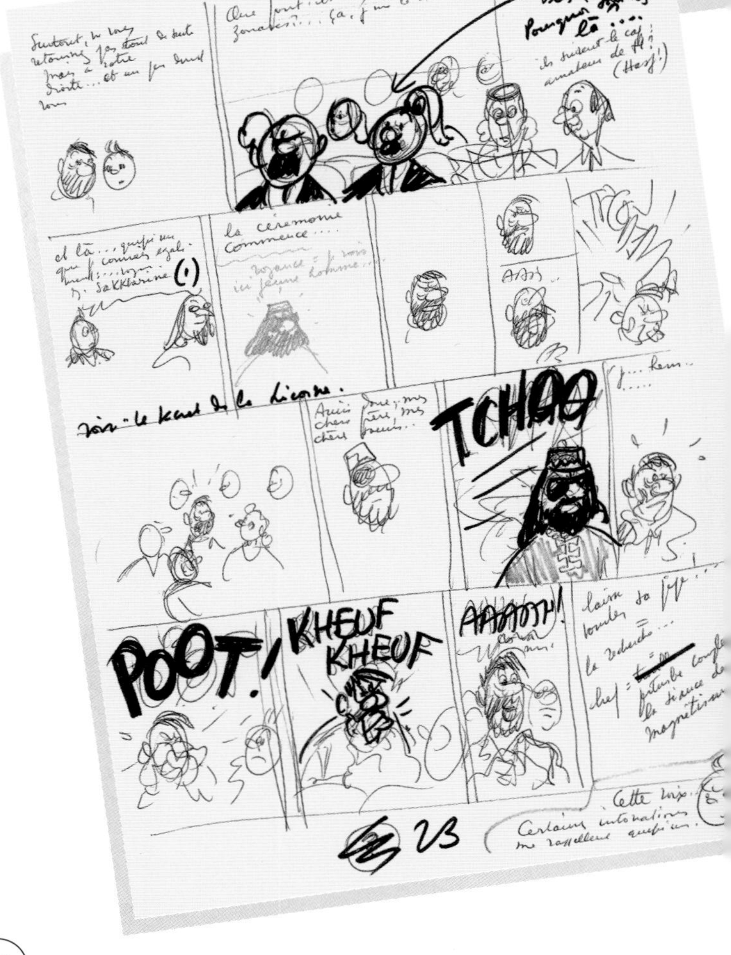
TCHAA
POOT!
KHEUF
KHEUF
23

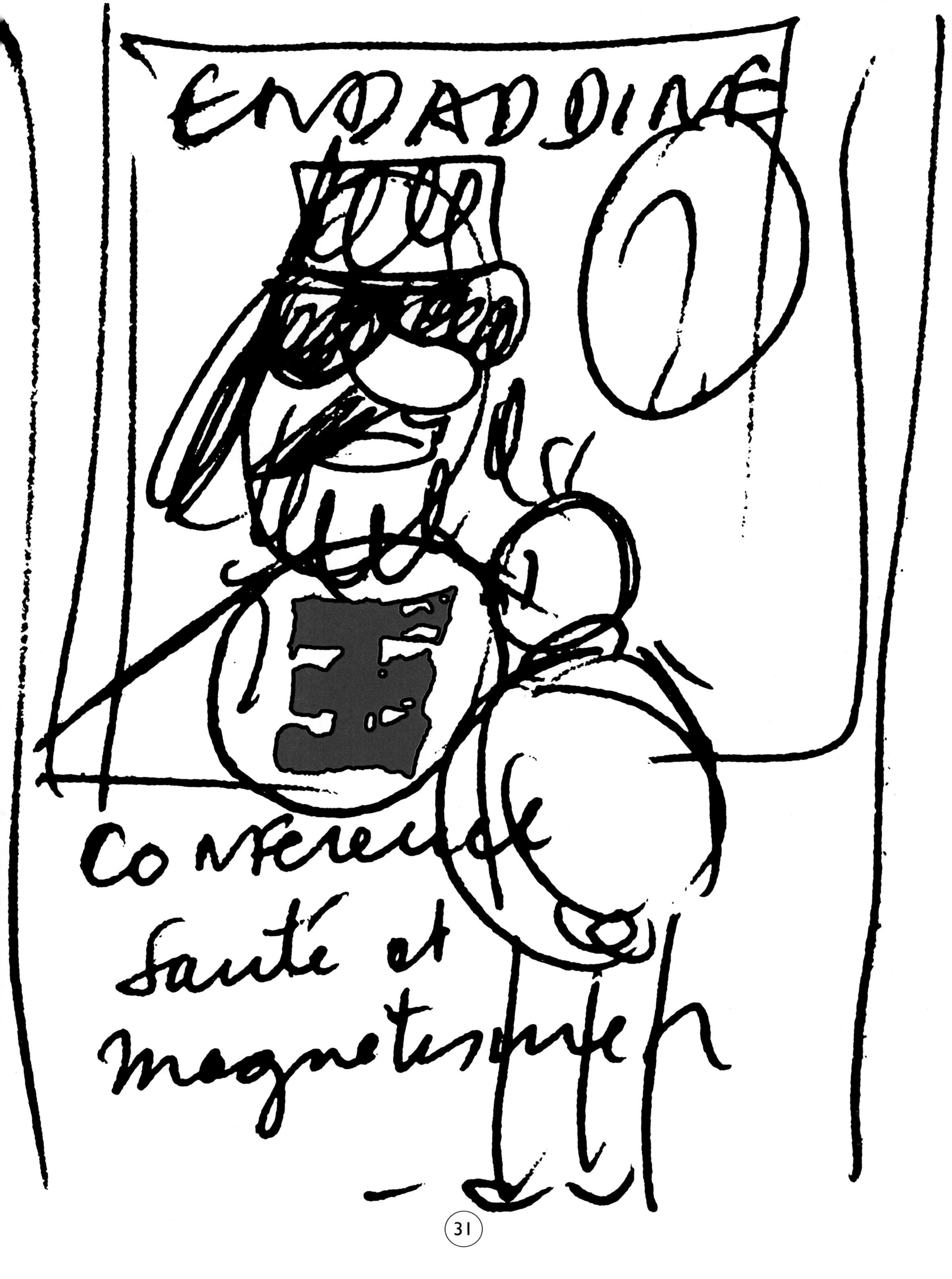
Santé et

The double trap...

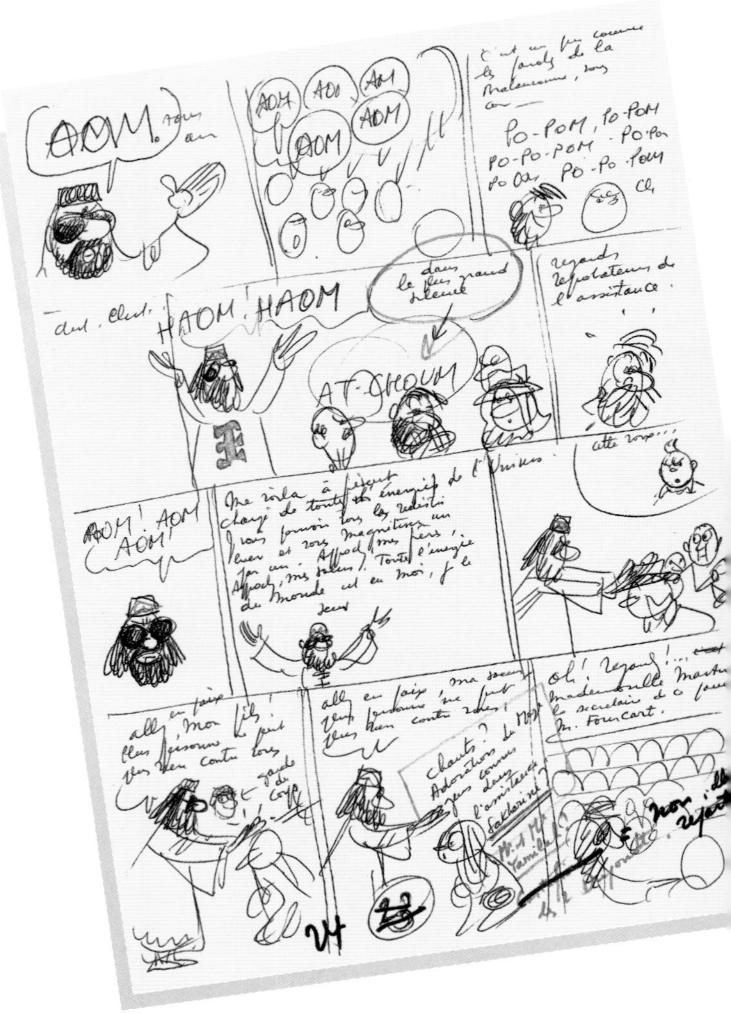
AOM
HAOM! HAOM
AT-CHOUM
AOM! AOM
AOM

When order is fully restored, the master utters the magic syllable.

ENDADDINE: AOM!

THE AUDIENCE: AOM, AOM, AOM, AOM...

HADDOCK: It's a bit like the Marlinspike village band. You know: PO-POM, PO-POM, PO-PO-POM, PO-POM, PO-POM, PO-PO-POM...

TINTIN: Ssh!

Having produced a last booming AOM, the mystic imposes silence with a grand gesture. At that moment, the Captain gives vent to another particularly sonorous sneeze. He blows his nose again, under the disapproving gaze of the audience.

ENDADDINE: AOM! AOM! AOM! Now I am filled with all the powers of the Universe. I am going to pass them to you, and magnetise you one by one. Draw near, my brothers, draw near, my sisters! All the energy in the world is in me, I feel it...

TINTIN: That voice... Some of his intonations remind me of... of... someone. But who?

The audience begins to move forward for the laying on of hands. One by one they kneel before the master.

ENDADDINE: Go in peace, my son! None may stand against you.

TINTIN: Oh, look! Miss Martine, poor Mr Fourcart's assistant. She's leaving... Come on, we'll follow her...

HADDOCK: I say, you...

They leave the hall.

TINTIN: There she is! *(Hurrying to catch up with her)* Good evening, Miss Martine.

MARTINE: Oh, it's you... and Mr Kodak?...

HADDOCK: Haddock, madam.

MARTINE: How do you happen to...

TINTIN: Oh, we were passing this way. And since I'd heard about Endaddine from a friend...

MARTINE: Ah, yes... He's a wonderful man, you know!... He magnetises people...

TINTIN: Yes, yes, I saw... And he gave you that jewel?

MARTINE: Yes... At least I bought it from him and he magnetised it for me... It's a real talisman... I keep it with me always.

TINTIN: May I? *(feeling the weight of the jewel)* It's superb. Oh, how heavy it is... Surely it must be gold.

MARTINE: Yes, I think it is.

TINTIN: It's beautiful. And what does the design mean?

MARTINE: There are two Es, back to back.

TINTIN: Ah, Alph-Art.

MARTINE: No, no. E is the initial of Endaddine.

TINTIN: Yes, that's true... May we take you home, Miss Martine?

MARTINE: Thank you, if it is on your way.

They take her with them and leave her at the door.

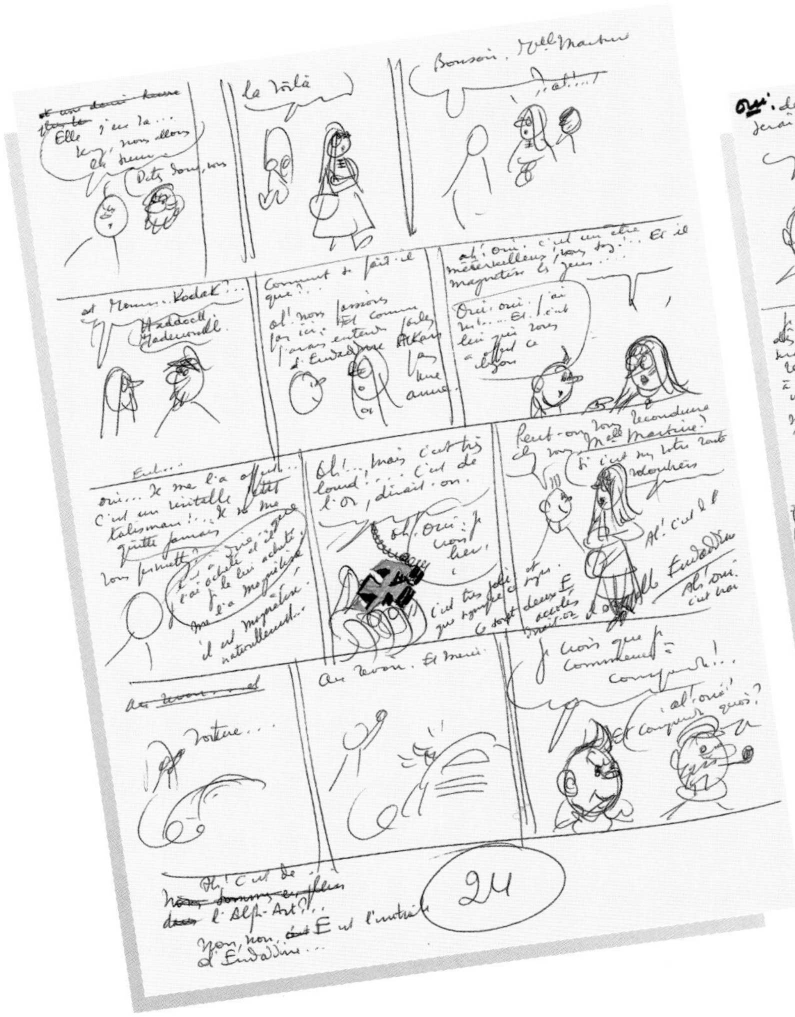
24

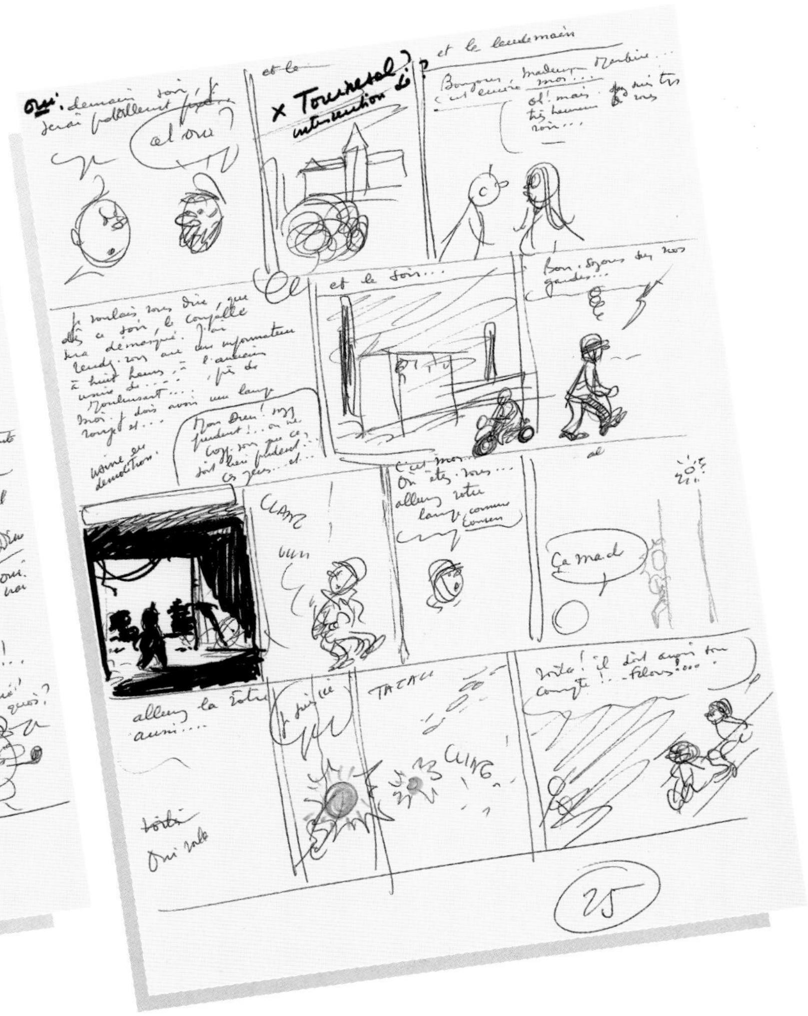
25

MARTINE: Goodbye, and thank you.

TINTIN: I think I'm beginning to understand!...

HADDOCK: Oh, yes? Understand what?

TINTIN: By tomorrow evening I shall probably have it all sewn up…

HADDOCK: Oh yes?

THE NEXT MORNING

TINTIN: Good morning, Miss Martine… It's me again…

MARTINE: Oh, but I'm always very glad to see you…

TINTIN: I want to tell you that by this evening the criminal will be unmasked. I have a rendezvous with an informer at eight o'clock at the old Fréaux factory, near Marlinspike… You know, the one they're knocking down… I shall be carrying a red lamp and…

MARTINE: Goodness gracious! Be careful!...

THAT EVENING

TINTIN *(parking his scooter near the entrance to the disused factory)*: Good! Now I must be on my guard… *(Scarcely has he entered the building than he hears a metallic sound behind him)* It's me… Where are you? Light your red lamp, as we agreed! *(A red lamp glows in the darkness)* That'll do.

A VOICE: You light yours, too.

TINTIN: Yes, there… I'm here.

The response is an immediate burst of automatic gunfire. Tintin falls to the ground. Two shadowy figures disappear into the darkness.

A VOICE: Quick! He's had it! Let's get out!

Tintin investigates (cont'd)...

haut les mains!
26

TINTIN *(picking himself up and waving his gun)*: Hands up!

But one of his attackers has crept round behind and knocks him cold with a massive blow to the head. He wakes up in hospital. The Captain is at his bedside.

HADDOCK: You gave us a rare old fright. It was Snowy who alerted us.

TINTIN: Oh, my poor head! But at least I now know how the gangsters keep themselves informed about everything... A small, extremely sensitive electronic bug is hidden in the jewel.

HADDOCK: The jewel? What jewel?

TINTIN: The jewel worn by Miss Martine.

HADDOCK: All right, so what?

TINTIN: It's just a tiny microphone transmitter. That way, all conversations are recorded. Only...

HADDOCK: Only what?

TINTIN: Micro-transmitters like that have a very restricted range. So there must be some sort of relay nearby... Tomorrow I'll begin a search.

HADDOCK: Tomorrow?... Out of the question! The doctor has ordered at least a week's rest.

TINTIN: Oh, has he?

Thomas d'Hardymont
M. et M. Cléonage.
Mme Ve Tricot
Mlle Dory Faure

AND THE NEXT MORNING

With a brisk step, Tintin heads for the Fourcart Gallery.

TINTIN: Today, Snowy, we're conducting an opinion survey on... on what, exactly? On solar-powered heating? Yes, solar-powered heating, that's an excellent subject. *(He goes into the block of apartments which houses the gallery)* We'll start with the other tenants.

He examines the names of the occupants listed beside the bell pushes: Thomas d'Hartimont, Mr and Mrs Cléonage, Widow Tricot, Miss Dory Faure. He rings the bell for Mrs Tricot. A friendly, smiling woman opens the door, a baby in her arms.

TINTIN: Good morning, madam, I am conducting a survey about solar-powered heating. Would you be willing to answer a few questions?

MRS TRICOT: Come in, come in, young man.

Tintin comes out of the flat a while later, disappointed.

TINTIN: Nothing there, I think... Now for the flat next door... Patience, Snowy!

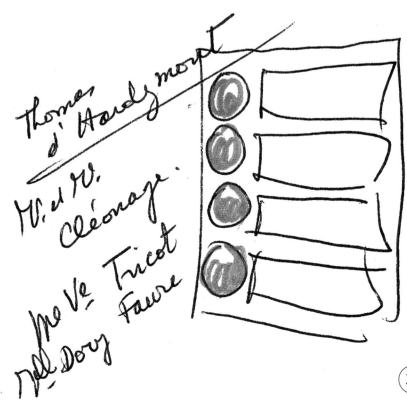

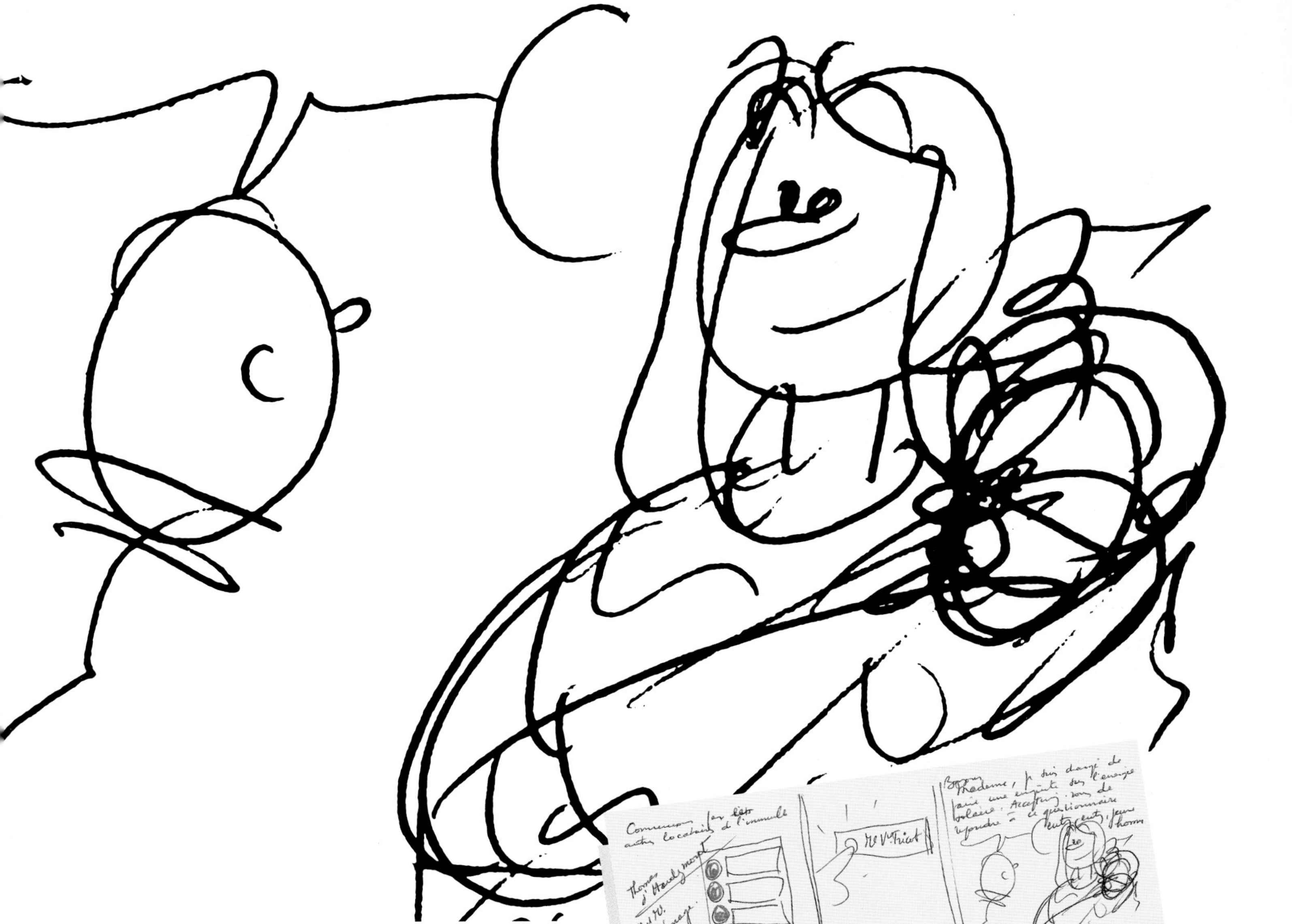

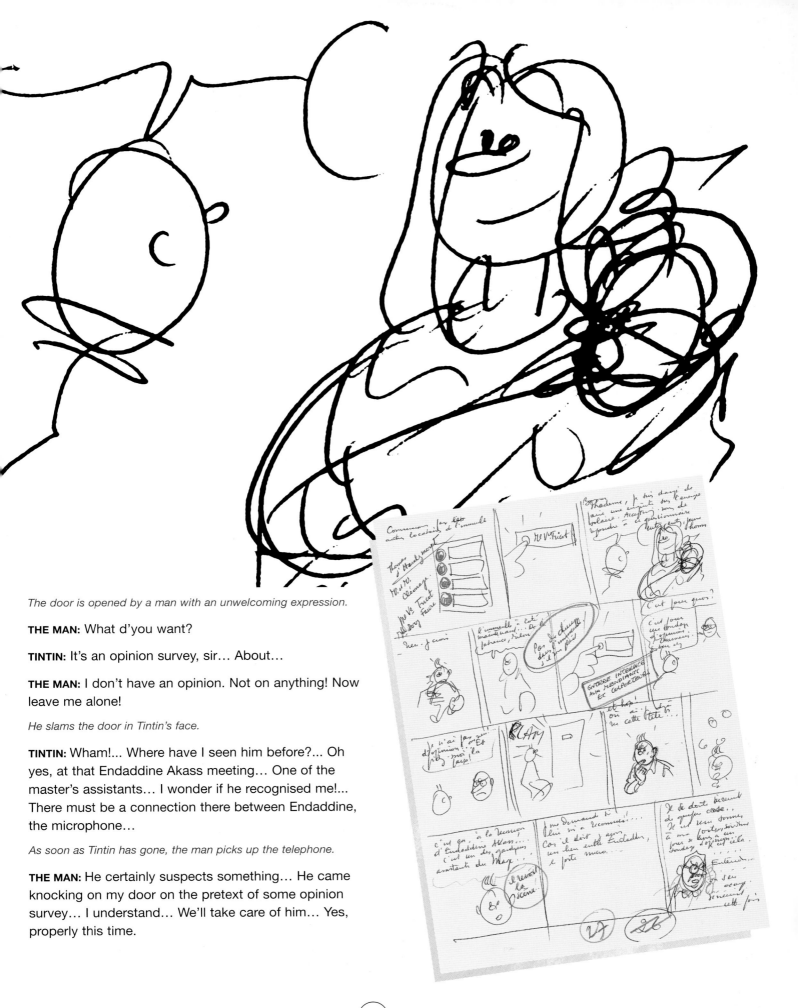

The door is opened by a man with an unwelcoming expression.

THE MAN: What d'you want?

TINTIN: It's an opinion survey, sir… About…

THE MAN: I don't have an opinion. Not on anything! Now leave me alone!

He slams the door in Tintin's face.

TINTIN: Wham!... Where have I seen him before?... Oh yes, at that Endaddine Akass meeting… One of the master's assistants… I wonder if he recognised me!... There must be a connection there between Endaddine, the microphone…

As soon as Tintin has gone, the man picks up the telephone.

THE MAN: He certainly suspects something… He came knocking on my door on the pretext of some opinion survey… I understand… We'll take care of him… Yes, properly this time.

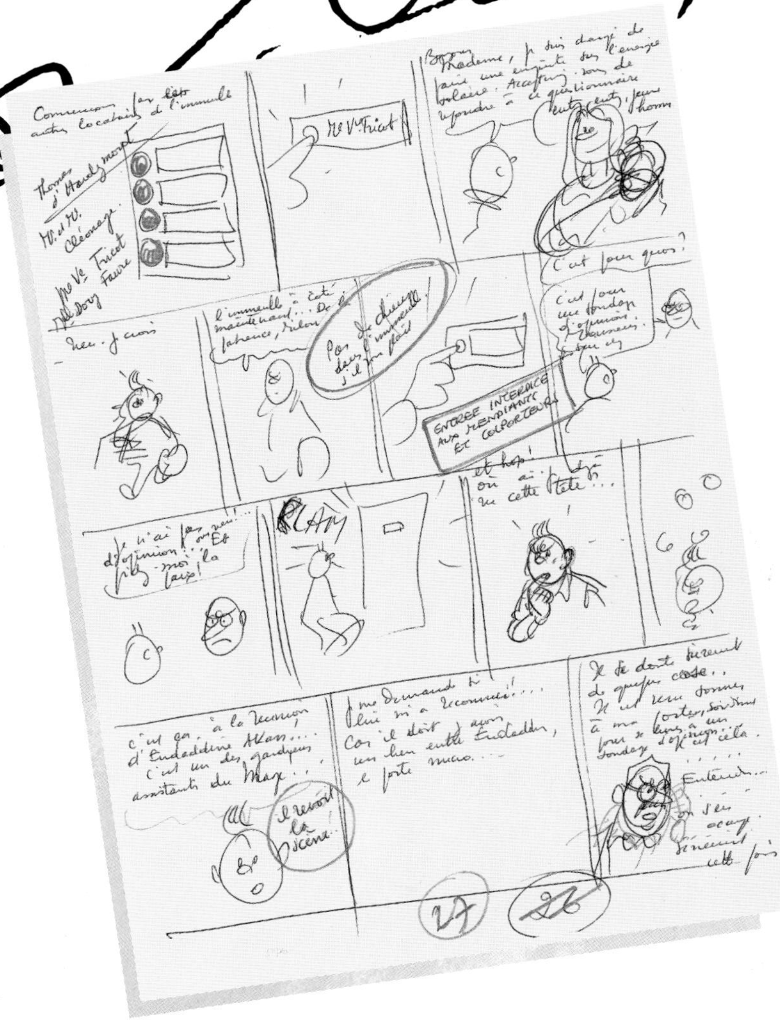
ENTREE INTERDICE
AUX MENDIANTS
ET COLPORTEURS

THE NEXT MORNING

In front of the steps at Marlinspike, Tintin has just mounted his scooter.

HADDOCK: Take care!... You never know, with those sort of people...

TINTIN: Don't worry, I'm only going into the village.

But a short distance from the house, Snowy suddenly starts to growl. Looking back, Tintin realises that a large car is coming after him.

THE DRIVER: There he is! We can get him!

TINTIN: They're going to catch me!

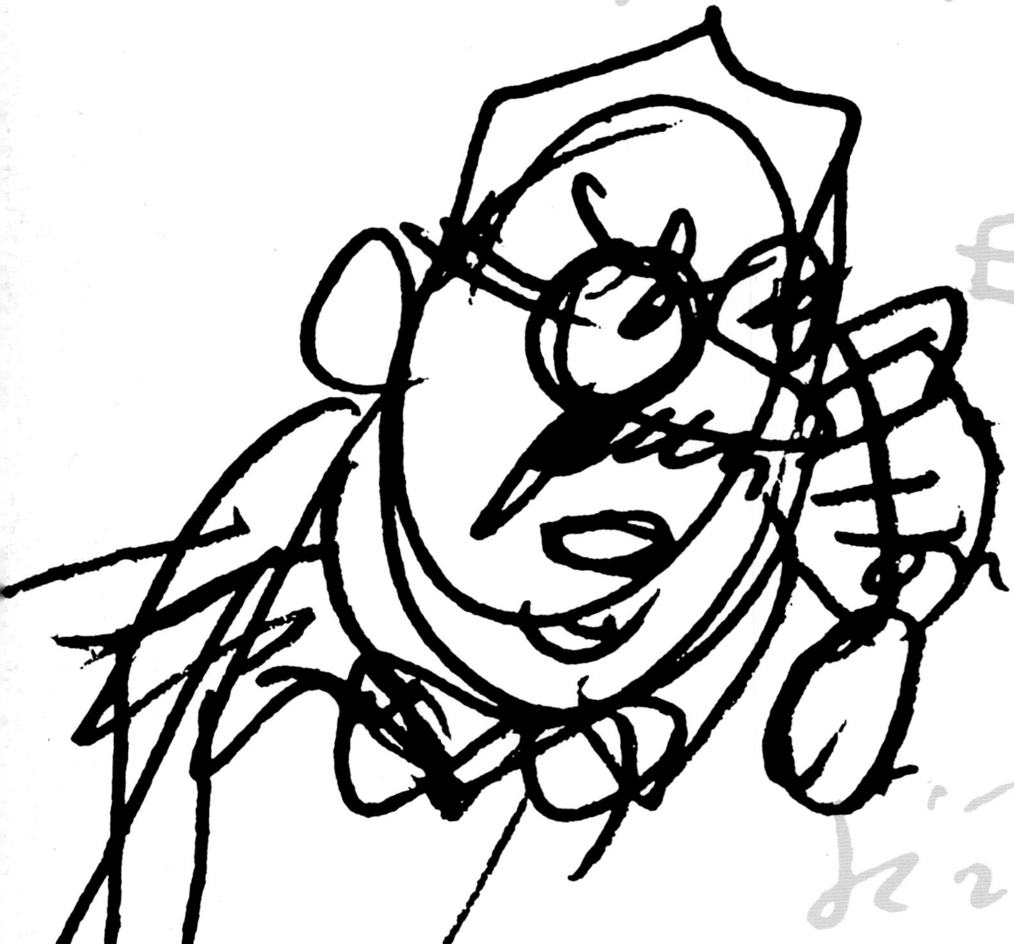

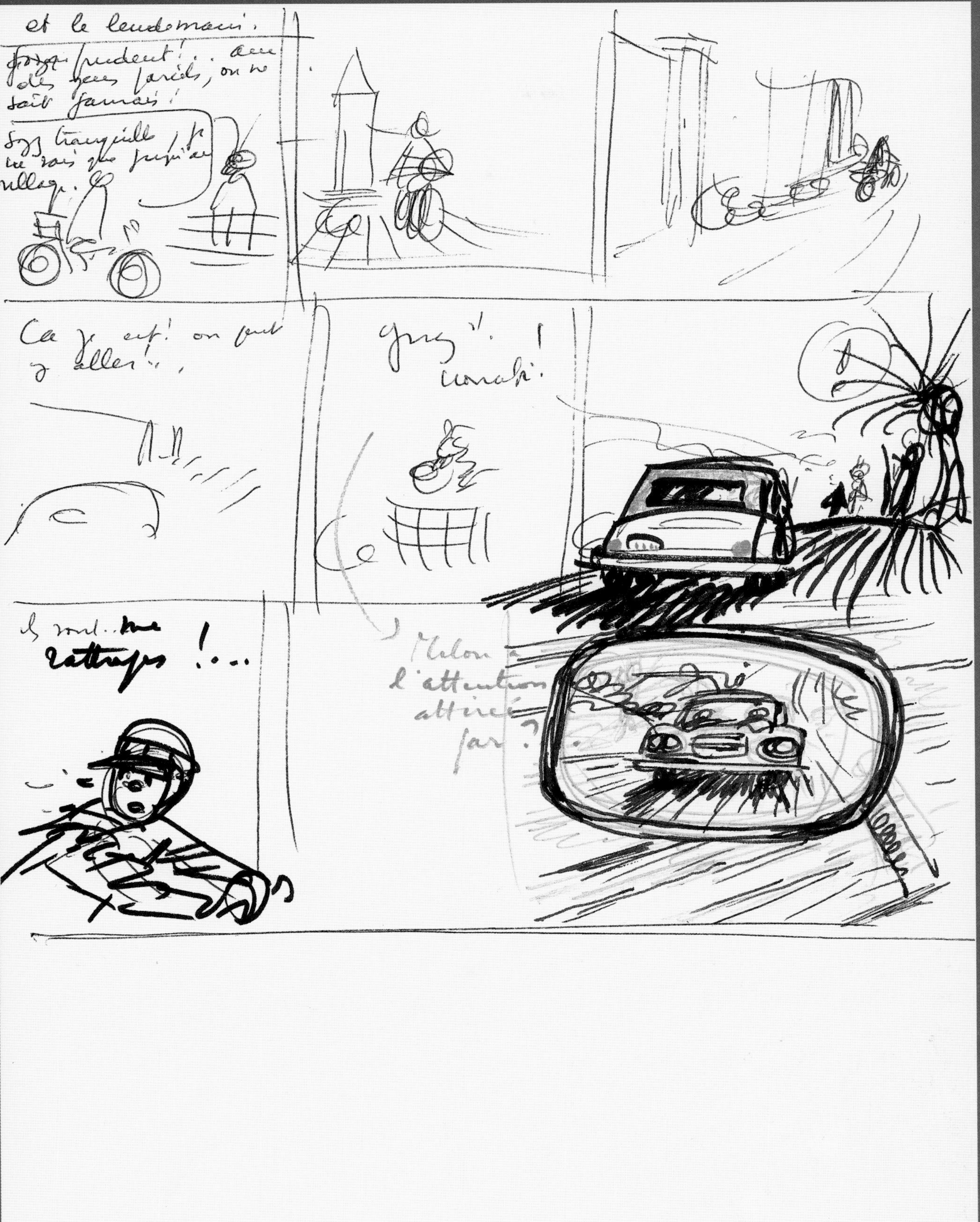

et le lendemain.
Ça y est! on peut y aller!..

Captured...

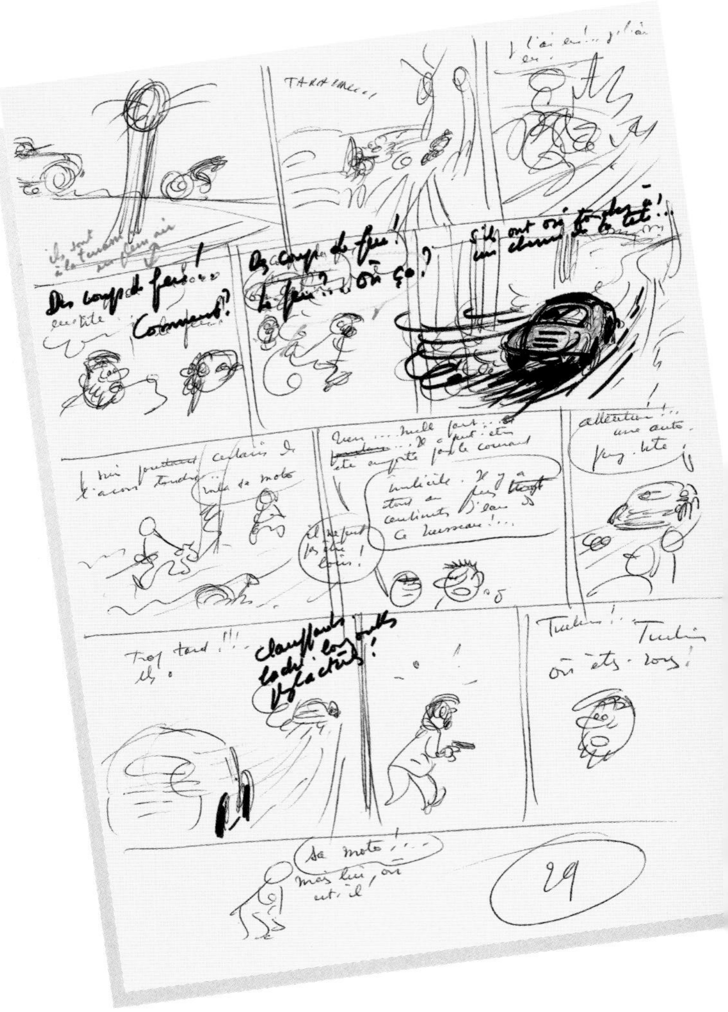

There is a burst of automatic gunfire. The scooter smashes into a tree.

ONE OF THE PURSUERS: I got him! I got him!

Up at the house, the Captain and Calculus are sitting on the terrace. The Captain jumps.

HADDOCK: Gunfire!

CALCULUS: What?

HADDOCK *(shouts)*: Gunfire!

CALCULUS: A fire? Where?

HADDOCK *(leaps into his car and takes off like a rocket)*: If they touch a hair of his head...

Some distance away, two men are searching both sides of the road.

FIRST MAN: I'm absolutely sure I hit him... There's his bike... Not a sign of him... He can't be far away... Nothing... Perhaps he was swept away by the current.

SECOND MAN: Imbecile! There are twenty centimetres of water at most in that stream... Look out, a car! Get going... quick!

HADDOCK *(pulls up abruptly)*: Too late, they've made off!... Roadhogs!... Bashi-bazouks! Phylloxera!

The gangsters' car has long since disappeared. The Captain, gun in hand, searches the roadside.

HADDOCK: Tintin!... Tintin!... Where are you? Ah, there's his scooter! But Tintin, where is he?

A VOICE: Is that you, Captain?

Looking up, the Captain sees Tintin in a tree where he has been hiding.

TINTIN: These pollarded willows sometimes come in handy, especially when they're hollow...

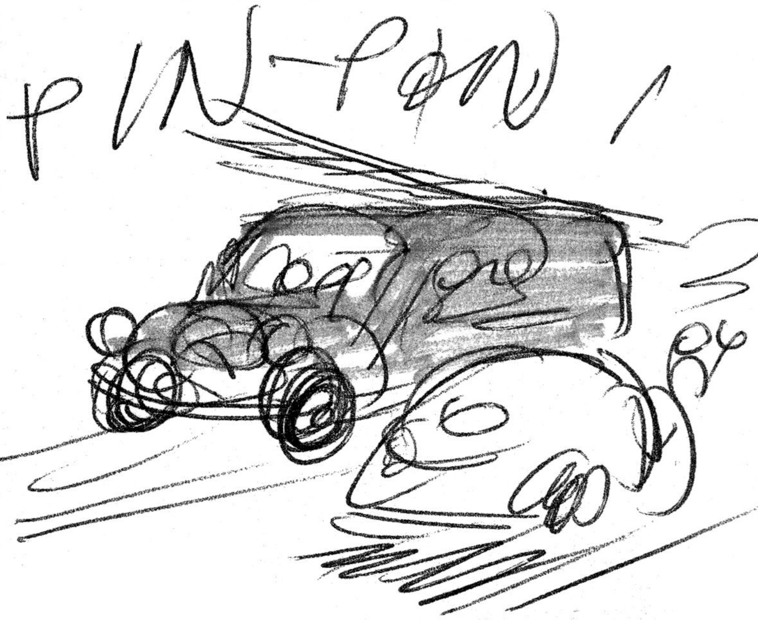
PIN-PON!

HADDOCK: Someone shot at you?

TINTIN: Yes, it's a habit... And this time they almost succeeded... Ssh! Listen...

In the distance a characteristic wailing note can be heard.

TINTIN: The fire brigade!

A fire engine appears, hurtling towards Marlinspike. Tintin and the Captain leap into their car in hot pursuit.

HADDOCK: They're going to the Hall...

The firemen jump out of their vehicle and run towards the house, closely followed by Tintin and the Captain.

A FIREMAN: Where is it, where's the fire?

HADDOCK: There's a fire? What fire?

A FIREMAN: Yes, someone called us to report a fire here...

Calculus appears at the top of the steps outside the front door.

CALCULUS: Ah, there you are, gentlemen... I sent for you. We have a fire. The Captain told me so.

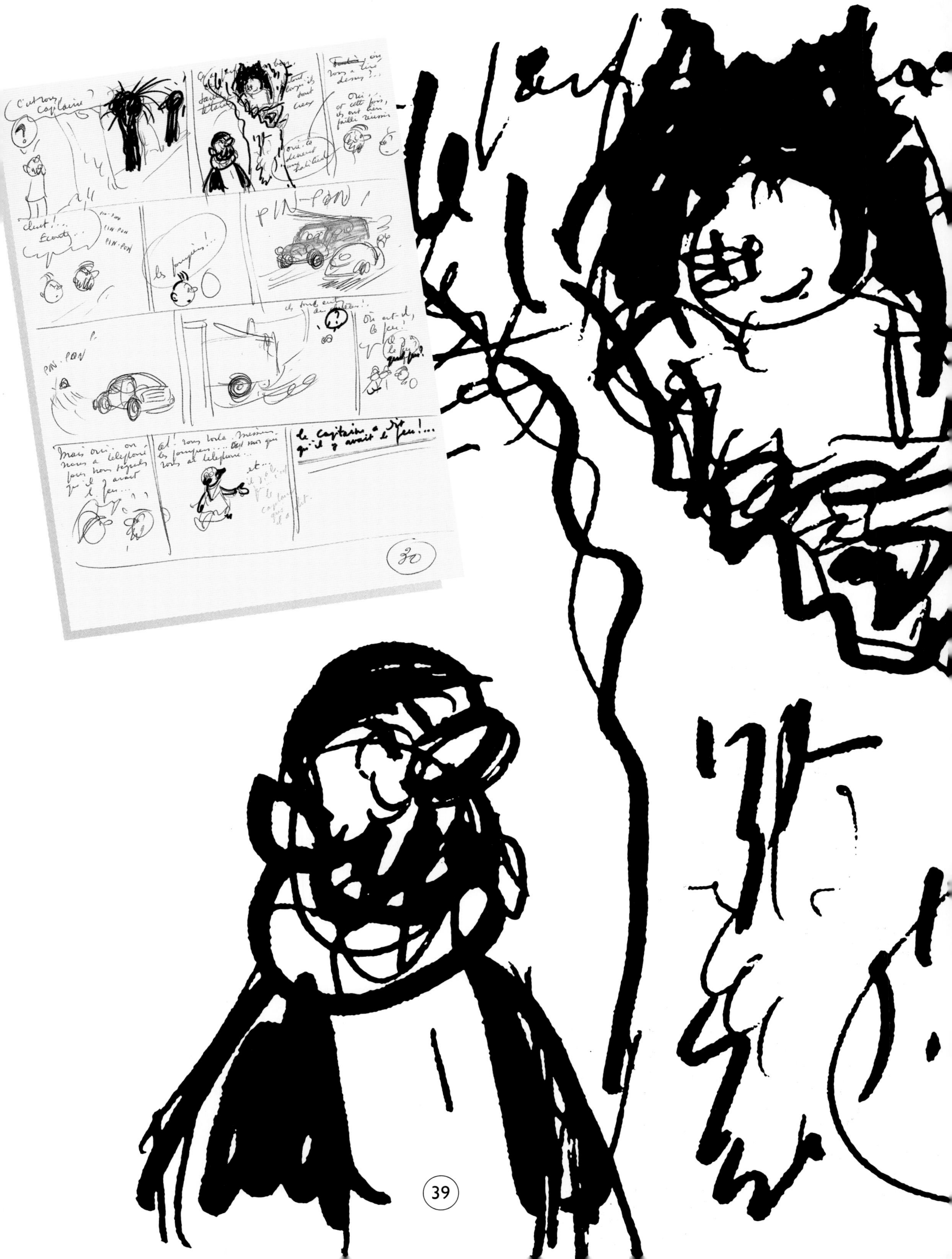
PIN-PON !
PIN-PON
Où est-il, le feu ?
Mais oui... on nous a téléphoné pour nous signaler qu'il y avait le feu...
le capitaine a dit qu'il y avait le feu !...
30

Ischia...

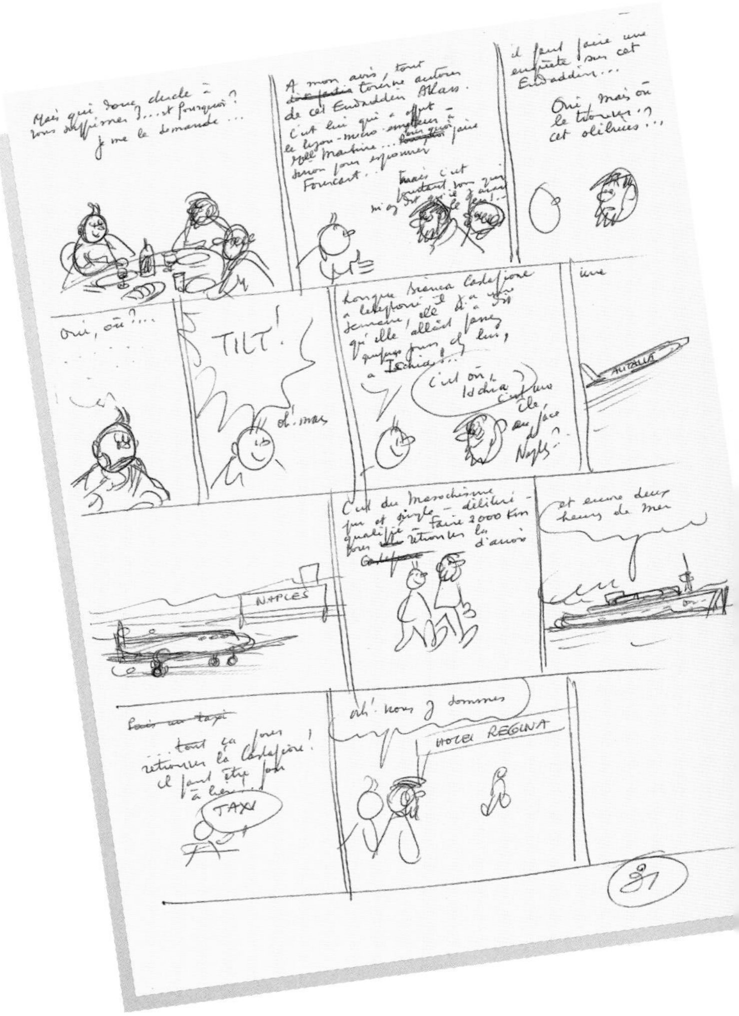
TILT!
NAPLES
HOTEL REGINA
TAXI

The misunderstanding sorted out, Tintin, the Captain and Calculus take stock round the table.

HADDOCK: But who is trying to get rid of you? And why? I wonder…

TINTIN: To my mind, it all revolves around that Endaddine Akass. He planted that jewel-microphone transmitter on Miss Martine… What for, if it wasn't to spy on Fourcart?

CALCULUS: But it was definitely you who told me there was a fire!

TINTIN: We must discover more about Endaddine…

HADDOCK: Yes, but where can we find him, the overdressed windbag?

TINTIN: Yes, where?... Great snakes, I've got it!... When Bianca Castafiore telephoned last week she told me that she was going to spend a few days with him, on Ischia.

HADDOCK: Where's Ischia?

TINTIN: It's an island across from Naples.

Some hours later, an airliner lands at Naples airport.

HADDOCK: This is sheer, deliberate, unqualified masochism, to come 2,000 kilometres by air…

TINTIN: And another two hours by sea!

HADDOCK: …all to find Castafiore!... We must be raving mad!

The two travellers arrive at their destination, the Hotel Regina, and make their way to the reception desk.

TINTIN: Tintin and Haddock. We made a reservation.

THE RECEPTIONIST: Indeed… Welcome to Ischia, Signore!

TINTIN: Please… we need a little information… Can you tell me where to find the villa belonging to Mr Endaddine Akass?

THE RECEPTIONIST: That's easy, Signore. I will show you. *(He leads them outside and points to a villa on top of the hill. Fortissimo strains of 'Ah, these jewels bright I wear', wafting down, tell them all they need to know)* There, that is the villa of Signor Endaddine Akass… The famous diva has just arrived there.

TINTIN: Well, let's take a look…

They head towards the villa and take cover nearby. The Captain produces a pair of binoculars and begins to survey the house.

HADDOCK: Blistering barnacles! Ramó Nash!

TINTIN: Ramó Nash?

HADDOCK: Yes, the high priest of Alph-Art, creator of the H that I bought…

TINTIN: We must try to get into the house. I have a feeling… in there lies the key to this whole mysterious business. But how do we do that?

They return to the hotel and go up to their rooms.

HADDOCK: See you later!

TINTIN: See you later, Captain!

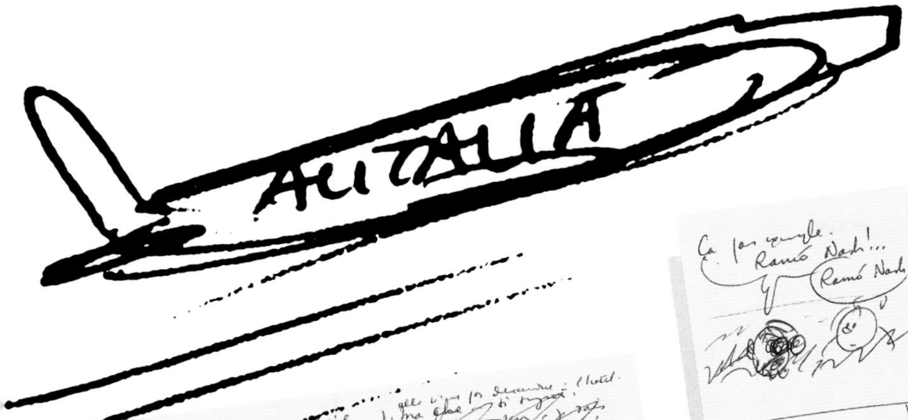
ALITALIA

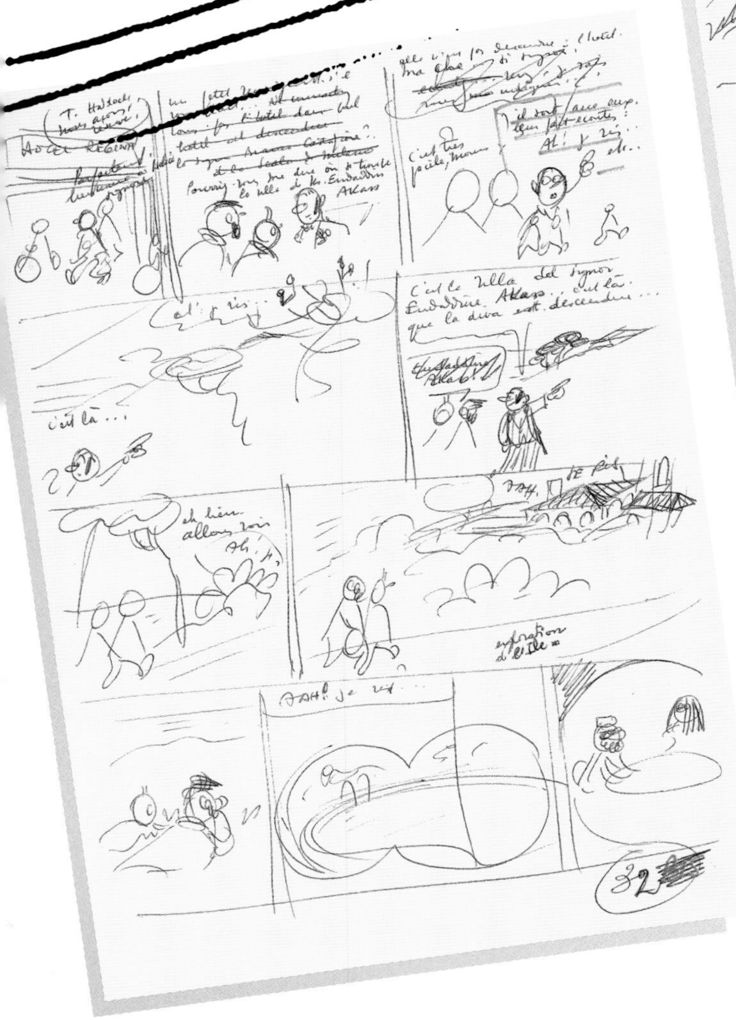
32

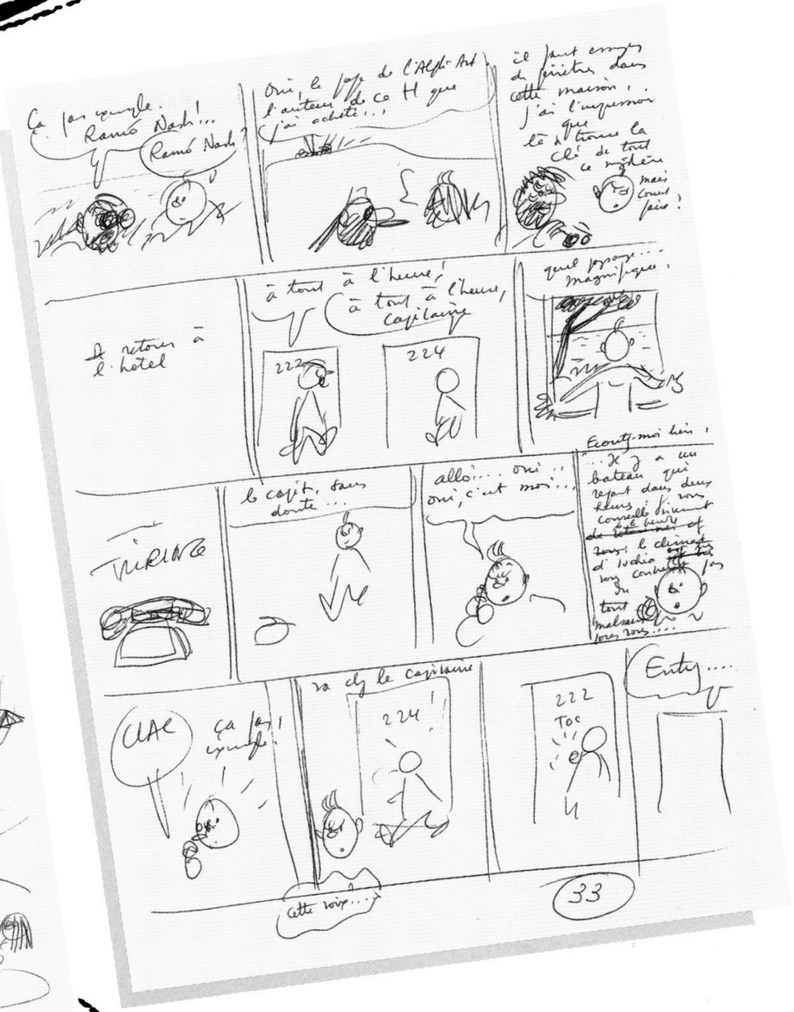
à tout à l'heure!
à tout à l'heure, capitaine
222
224
quel paysage... magnifique...
allô... oui... oui, c'est moi...
Entrez...
Toc
33

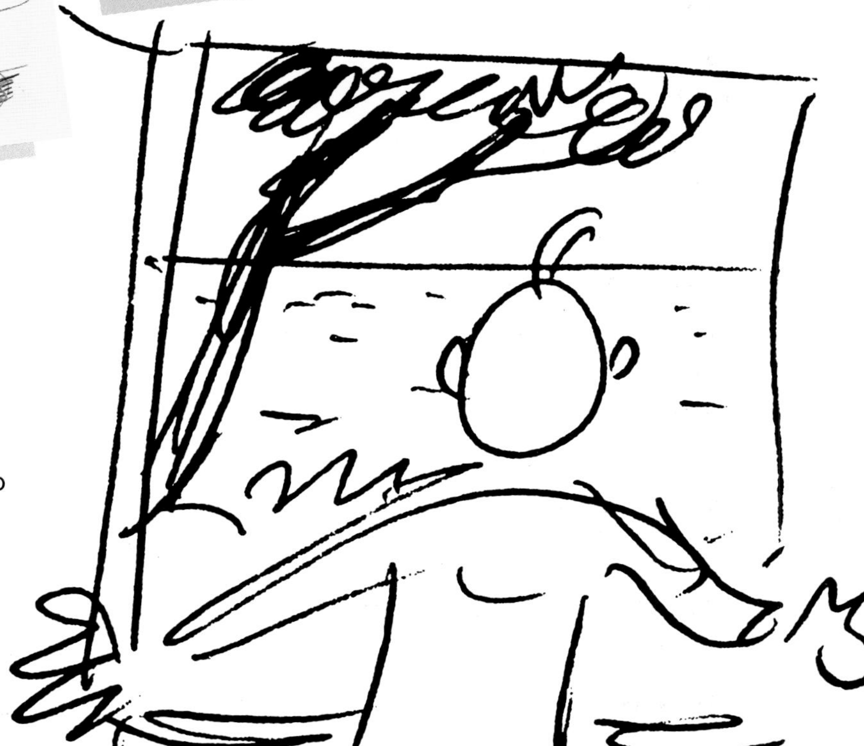

In his room Tintin opens the window wide.

TINTIN: What a marvellous view! *(The telephone rings)* The Captain, I expect… Hello… Yes… Yes, it is…

A VOICE: Listen carefully… there's a boat leaving in two hours. I strongly advise you to take it. The climate on Ischia doesn't suit you at all. It could even become very unhealthy for you! *(The telephone is slammed down)*

TINTIN: Crumbs!... That voice?... *(He leaves the room and knocks at the Captain's door)*

HADDOCK: Come in…

Introductions...

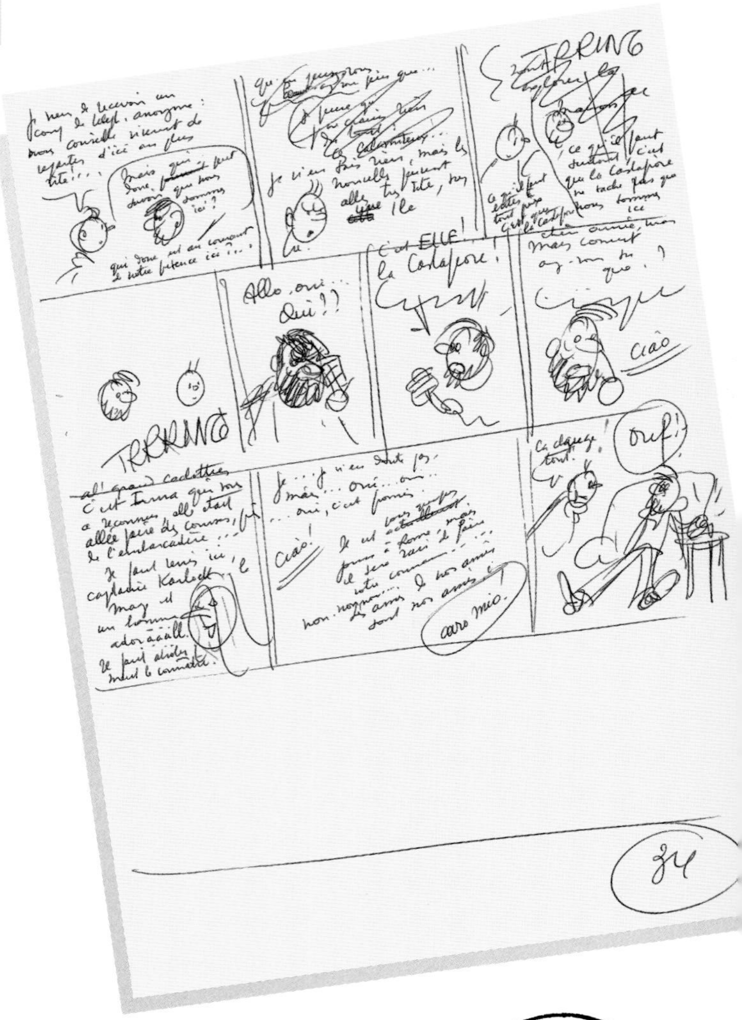
Allo, oui... Qui?
ciao
TRRRING
ouf!
caro mio
24

TINTIN: I've just received an anonymous telephone call. Someone strongly advises us to leave here... and fast...

HADDOCK: But who knows that we are here?

TINTIN: I've no idea, but news can travel very quickly on an island.

HADDOCK: The one thing we must avoid at all costs is Castafiore finding out we are here...

The telephone rings again. The Captain answers.

HADDOCK: Hello, yes... Who? *(To Tintin)* It's HER! Castafiore! *(To the singer)* My dear friend... but how did you know...?

CASTAFIORE: You old slyboots! Irma recognised you! She was taking a walk by the landing stage... You absolutely have to come here, Captain Karlock... The Master is the most ado-o-o-rable man. You absolutely have to meet him.

HADDOCK: I... I'm sure... But... Yes... yes... yes... I promise...

CASTAFIORE: He's gone to Rome for a few days, but he'll be delighted to meet you... No, no, no... The friends of our friends are our friends, caro mio!... Ciao!

HADDOCK *(hanging up)*: Phew!

TINTIN: That alters everything!

THE NEXT MORNING

A horse-drawn carriage takes Tintin and the Captain to the luxurious Villa Akass. A footman in livery shows them into an immense reception room where numerous guests are already assembled. Castafiore swoops forward to embrace them.

CASTAFIORE: My dear, dear friends, carissimi... Come, I simply must introduce you to everyone... *(She descends upon an elegant woman in dark glasses)* Darling, let me present Skipper Drydock, one of my closest friends... a real old sea-dog. This is Angelina Sordi...

HADDOCK: Madam! *(Just as the Captain is bowing low, Angelina waves her arm in a sudden, casual gesture; her hand smacks the unfortunate Captain hard in the face)*

CASTAFIORE: My dear friend, how could you have guessed that a simple seaman knew how to kiss hands?

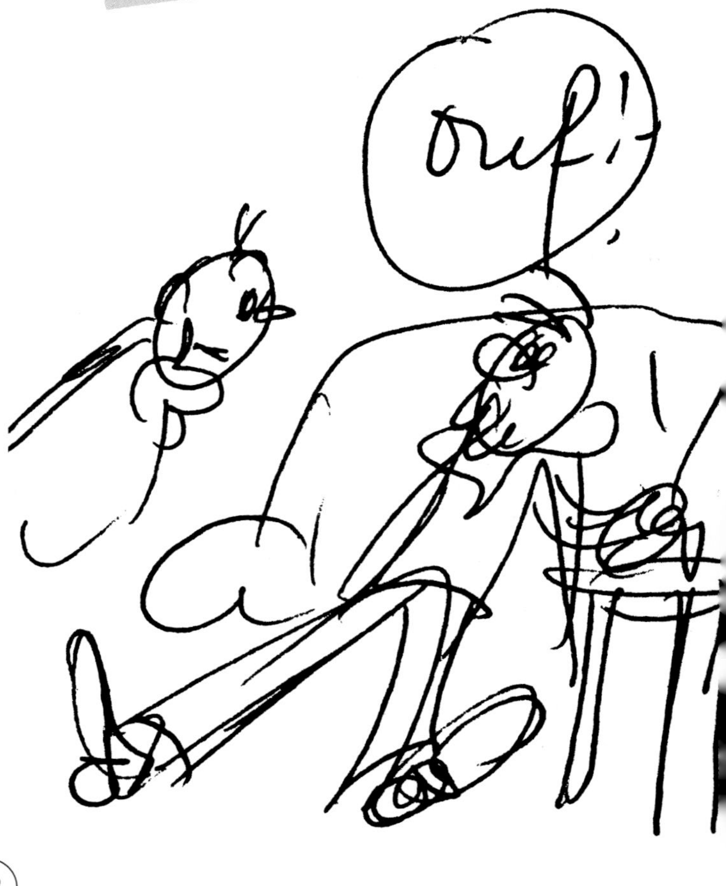
ouf!

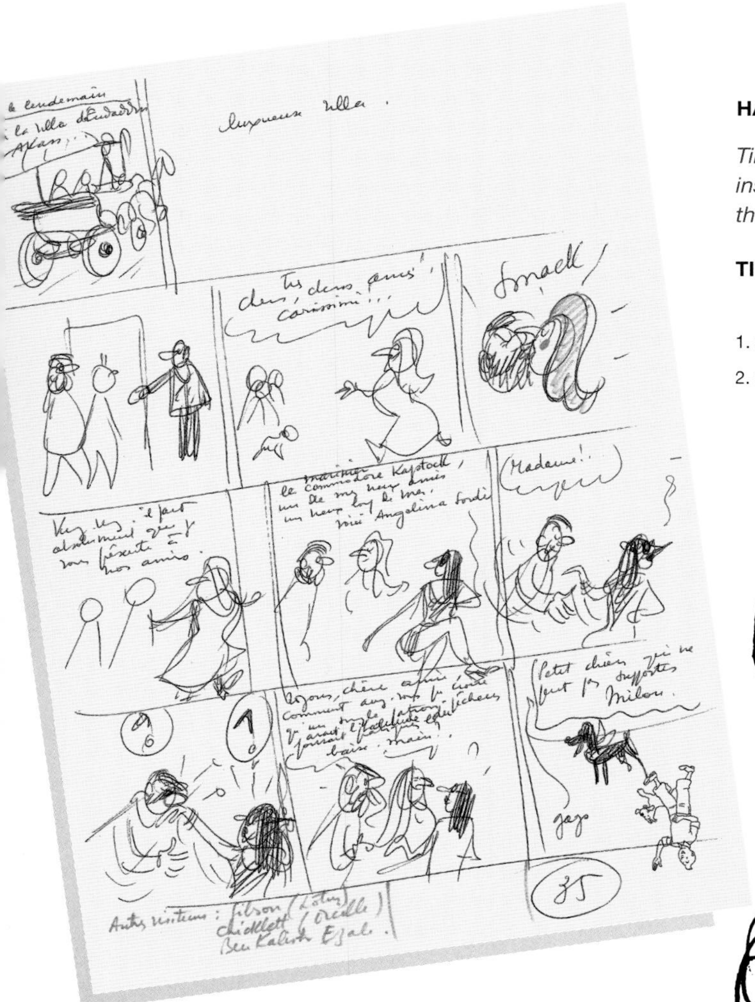

Meanwhile, Snowy approaches Castafiore's black miniature poodle.

SNOWY: What on earth is that?

THE POODLE: Who is this peasant?

SNOWY: Hello, beautiful!

Overcome by such familiarity, the poodle turns tail, squeaking loudly.

CASTAFIORE: My treasure! Come to me then, diddums! What did that big bully of a dog do to you?

SNOWY: There's justice for you!

The incident is closed. The introductions resume.

CASTAFIORE: This is Mr Gibbons, he's in import-export[1]... Mr Trickler, director of an important oil company[2]... Emir Ben Kalish Ezab... And Luigi Randazzo, a wonderful singer, as you are obviously aware...

HADDOCK: And how!

CASTAFIORE: And Ramó Nash, whom you already know...

The artist's latest work is hanging in the room: it consists of a gigantic Z, surrounded by a series of miniature Zs.

HADDOCK: Inspired!

Tintin himself is not mixing with the other guests. He discreetly inspects the room, noting especially the two servants, who have all the charm of gorillas.

TINTIN: What a peculiar smell!... It's as if... as if...

1. See *The Blue Lotus*

2. See *The Broken Ear*

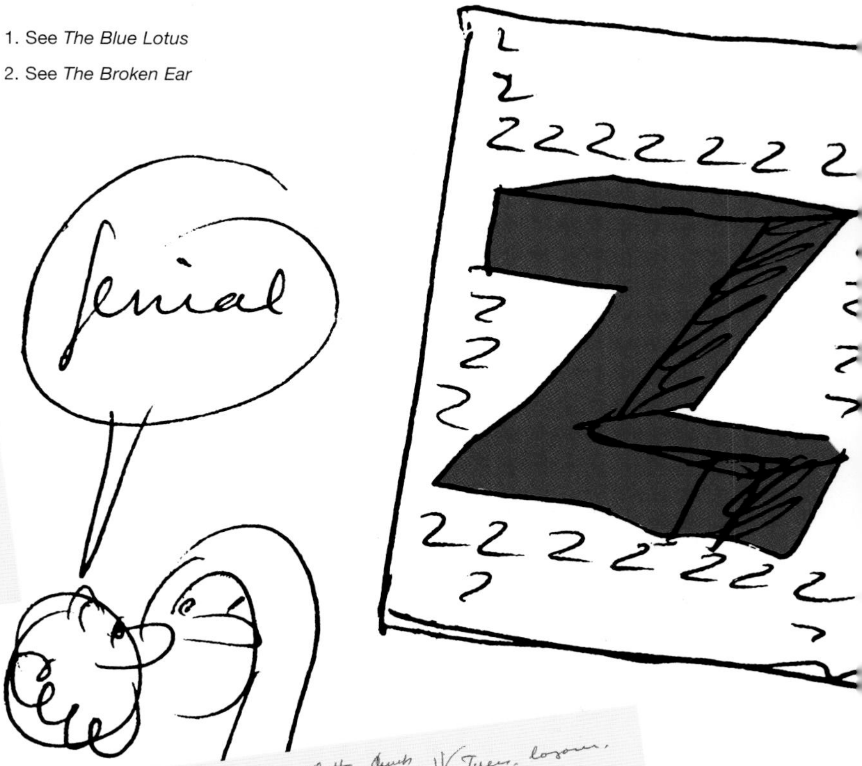

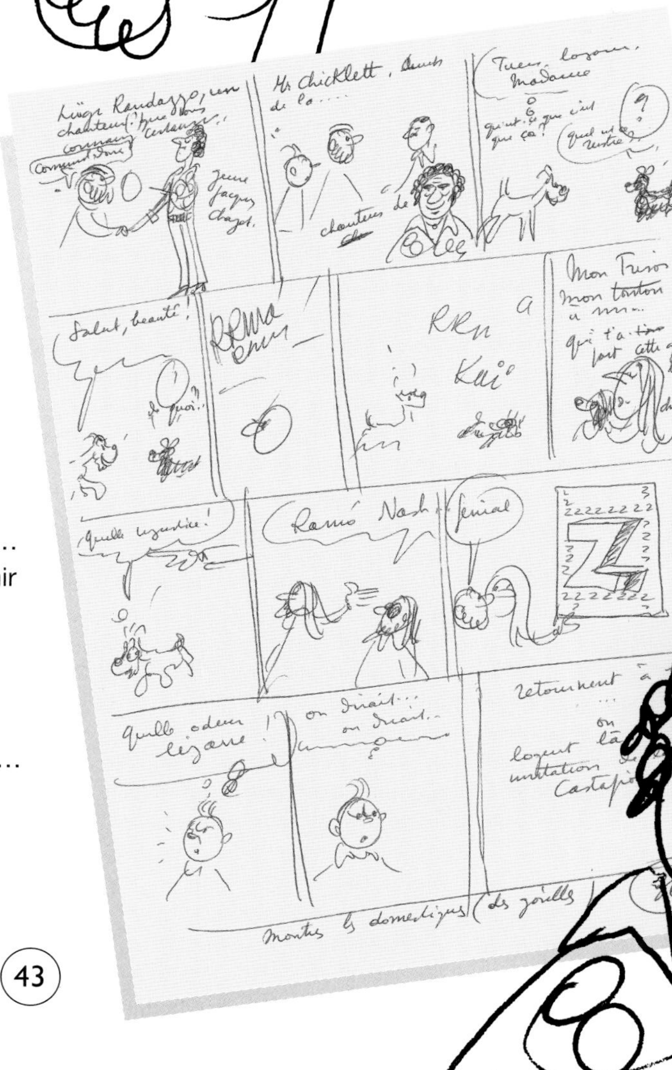

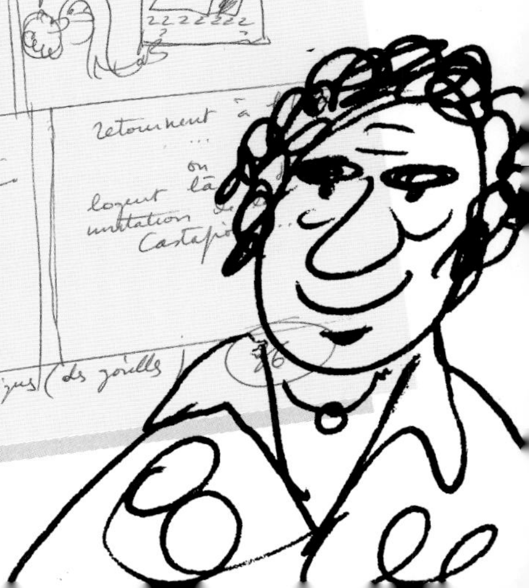

The reception is coming to an end. Some guests have already left.

HADDOCK: Well… Er… I think we'll go back to our hotel.

CASTAFIORE: But caro mio, it is out of the question. You must stay here tonight…

HADDOCK: But…

CASTAFIORE: Now, now… no fuss! *(she beckons to two large servants)* Please show these gentlemen to their rooms.

FIRST SERVANT: This is your room, Signor Tintin.

SECOND SERVANT: And this is yours, Signor… er… Pescatore.

They go to bed. But in the middle of the night Tintin is awakened by strange noises. He goes to the window and sees three men loading a van.

TINTIN: It looks as if… Yes, it looks as if they're loading pictures… or canvases… Why do it at the dead of night?

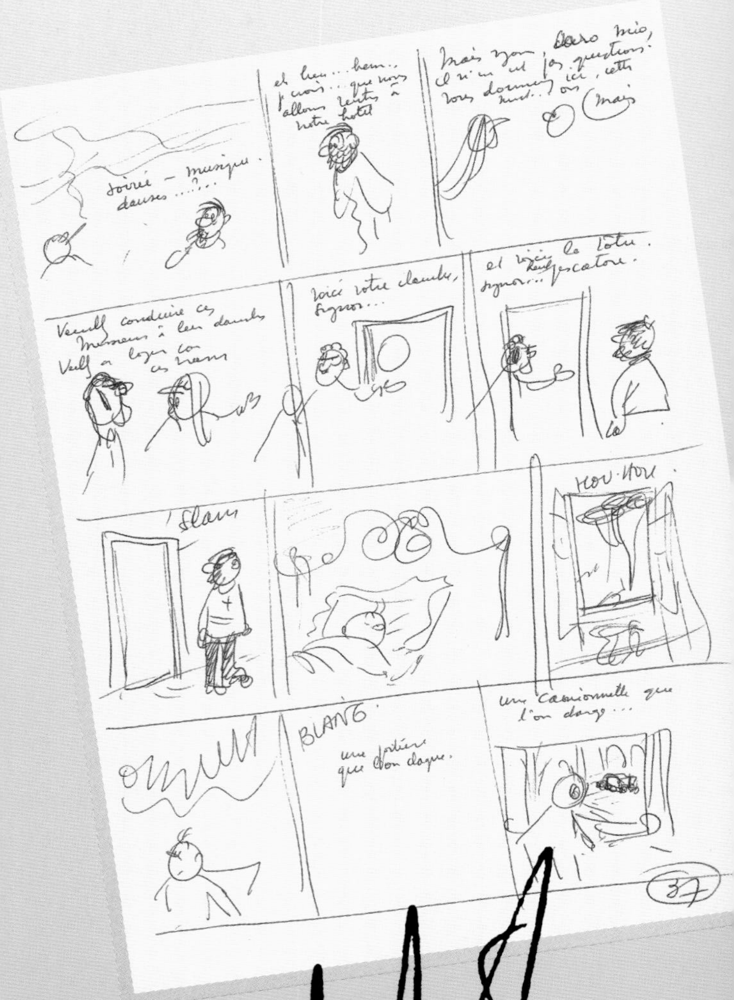

Slam
BLANG
une portière que l'on claque.
37

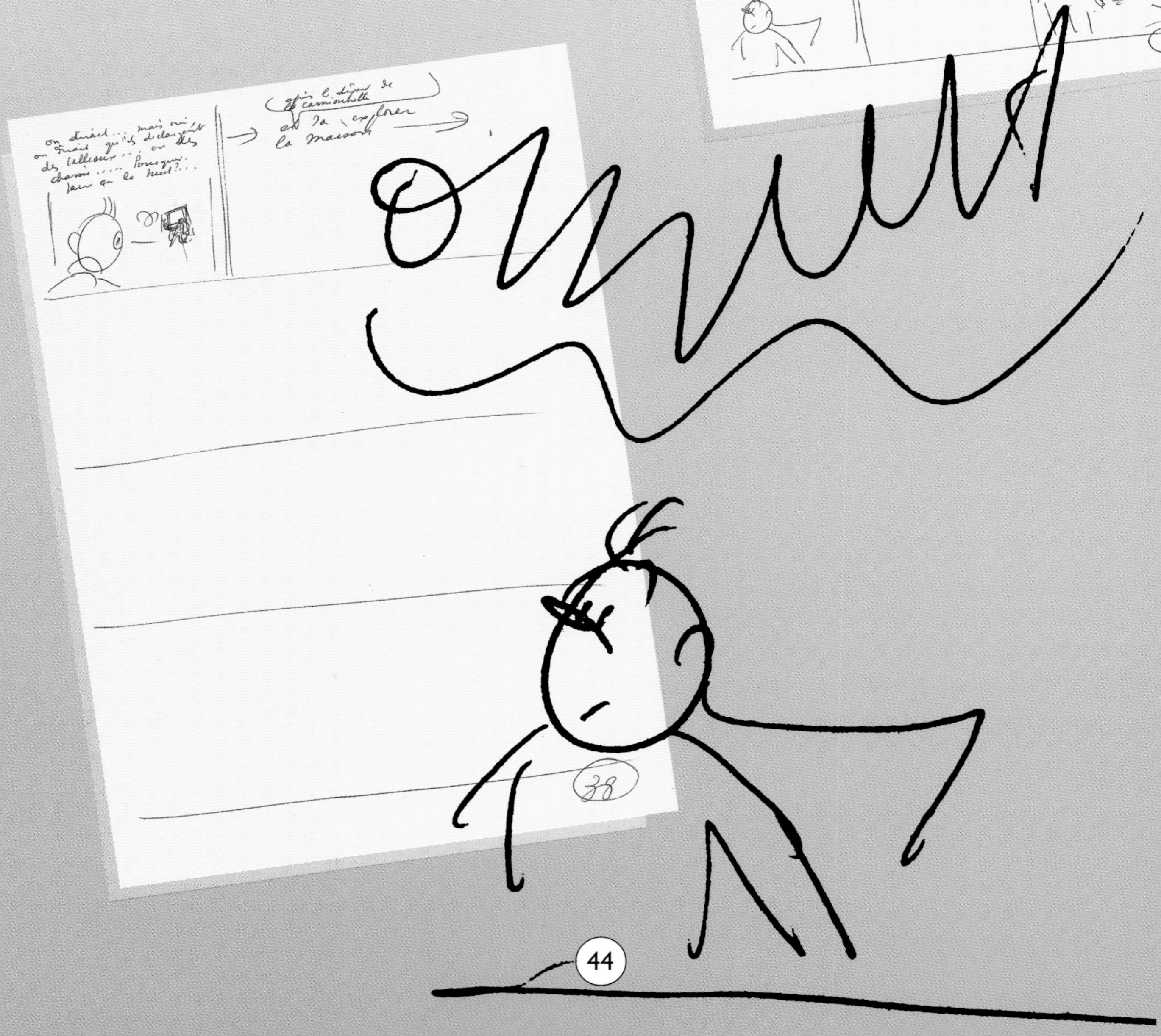

la maison
38

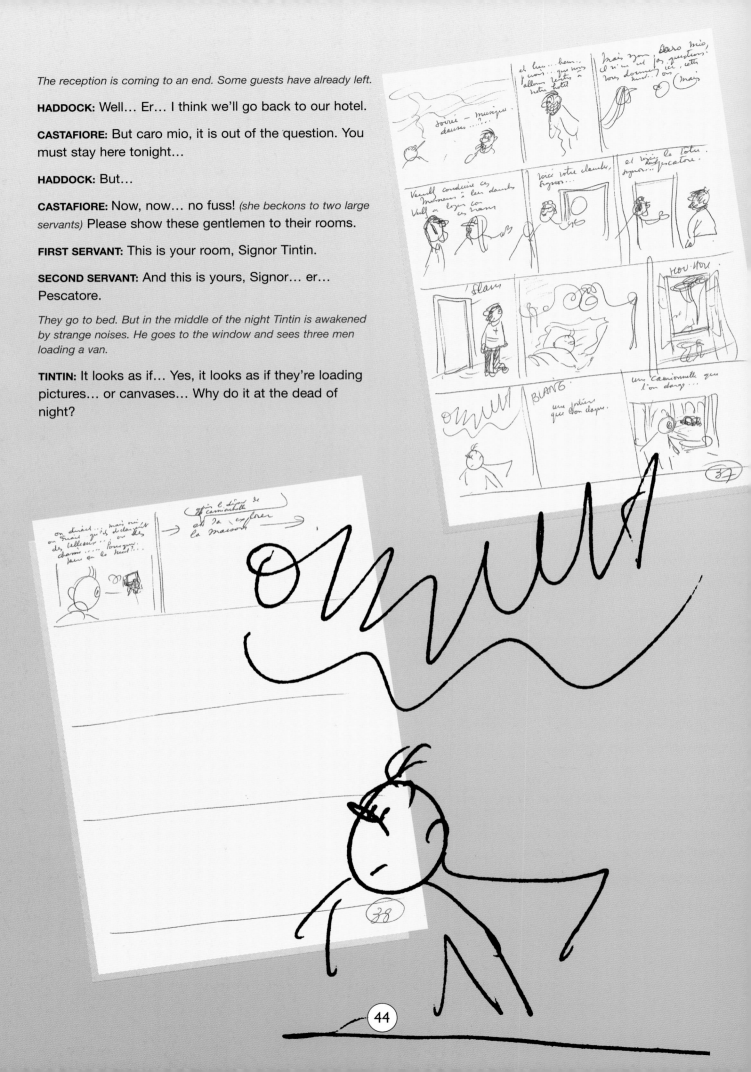

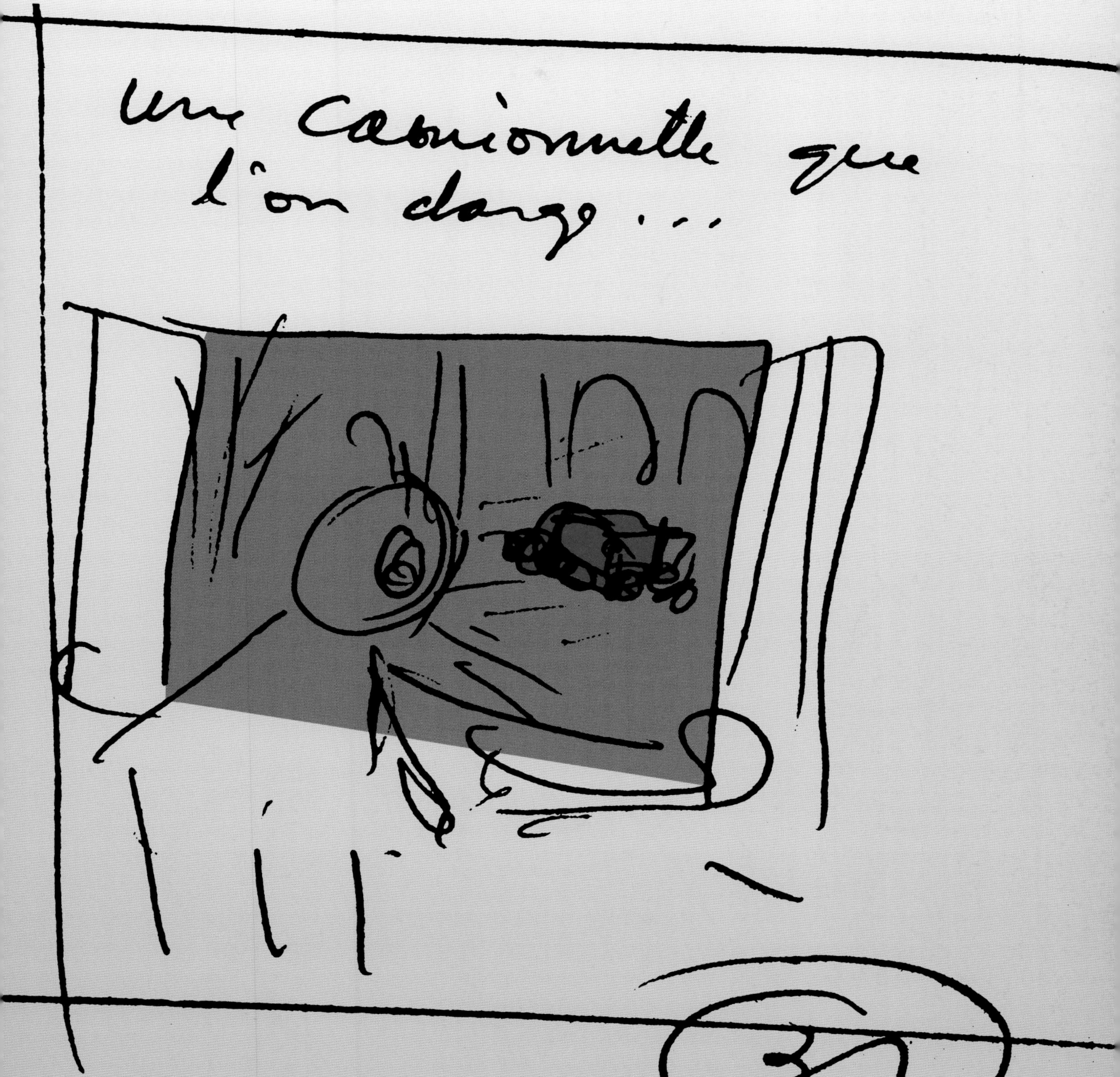
une camionnette que l'on charge...
37

When the van has departed, Tintin decides to explore the villa. Armed with a flashlight, he sets off through the corridors of the vast house. Suddenly he comes to a halt. In a huge room hang numerous pictures by great masters.

TINTIN: Oh! A Modigliani! *(He accidentally touches the canvas; a little paint comes off on his fingers)* It's still wet!... And here's a Léger… a Renoir… a Picasso… a Gauguin… a Monet… All fakes! A veritable factory for forging pictures, and perfect imitations, too! I wonder who…

A VOICE: Beautiful pictures, aren't they, my friend?

The lights go on. Endaddine Akass, flanked by his two bodyguards, stands facing Tintin.

TINTIN: Er… Certainly, whoever painted these has plenty of talent.

ENDADDINE: Oh, but you know him! It's our dear Ramó Nash. His latest brainwave is Alph-Art. Behind that front he can happily fabricate paintings by the masters. He has an extraordinary gift for imitation… Naturally, as soon as they are dry, these pictures will be authenticated by a known expert… Poor Mr Fourcart didn't want to accept our proposals. Besides, he wanted to expose the whole business to you. As for the unfortunate Monastir, he wanted to blackmail me. Poor fool!

TINTIN: You got rid of him…

ENDADDINE: I was forced to! As for you, young man, I'm desperately sorry, but you know too much. You will have to disappear. You know César?

TINTIN: Er… Caesar… Julius?

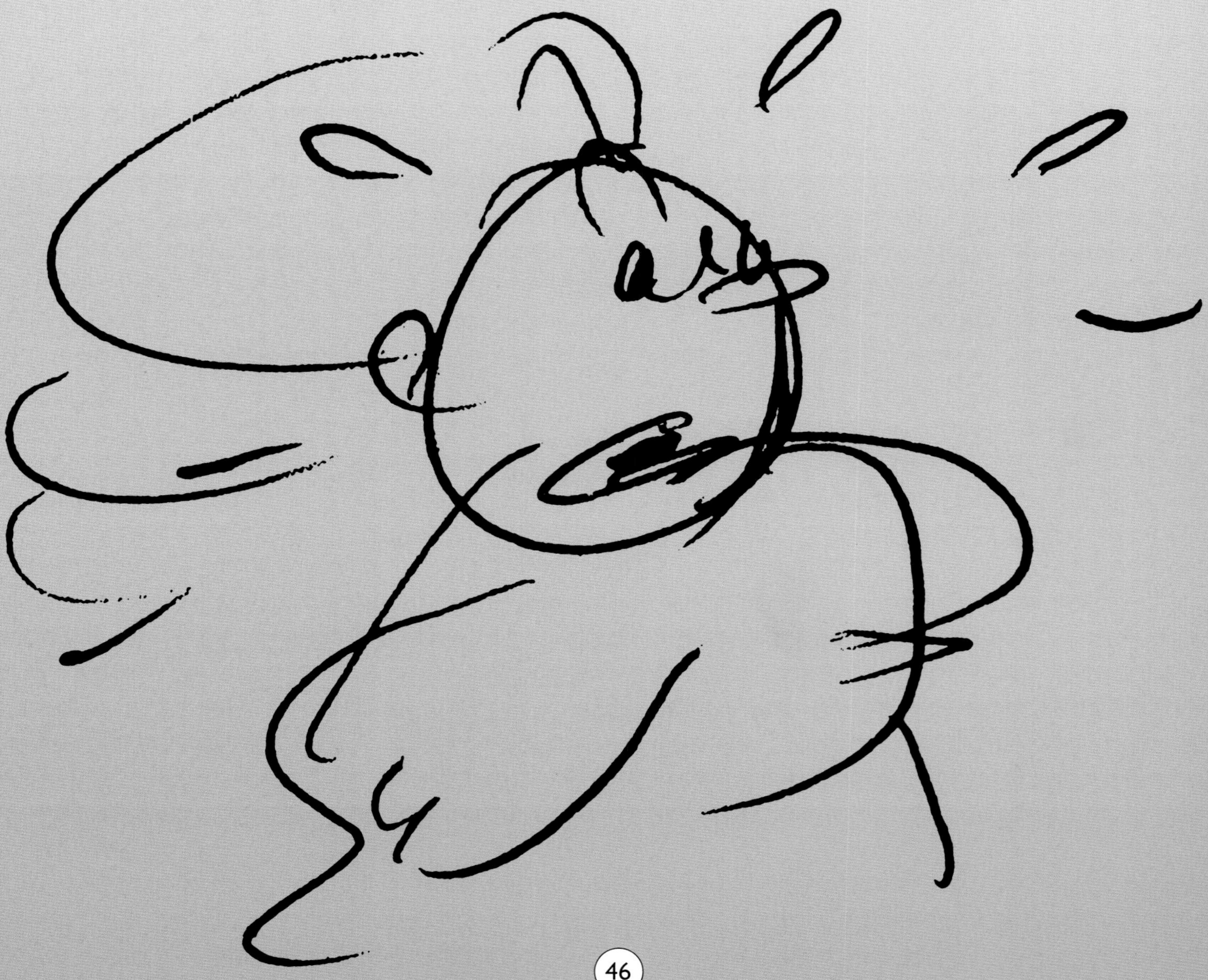

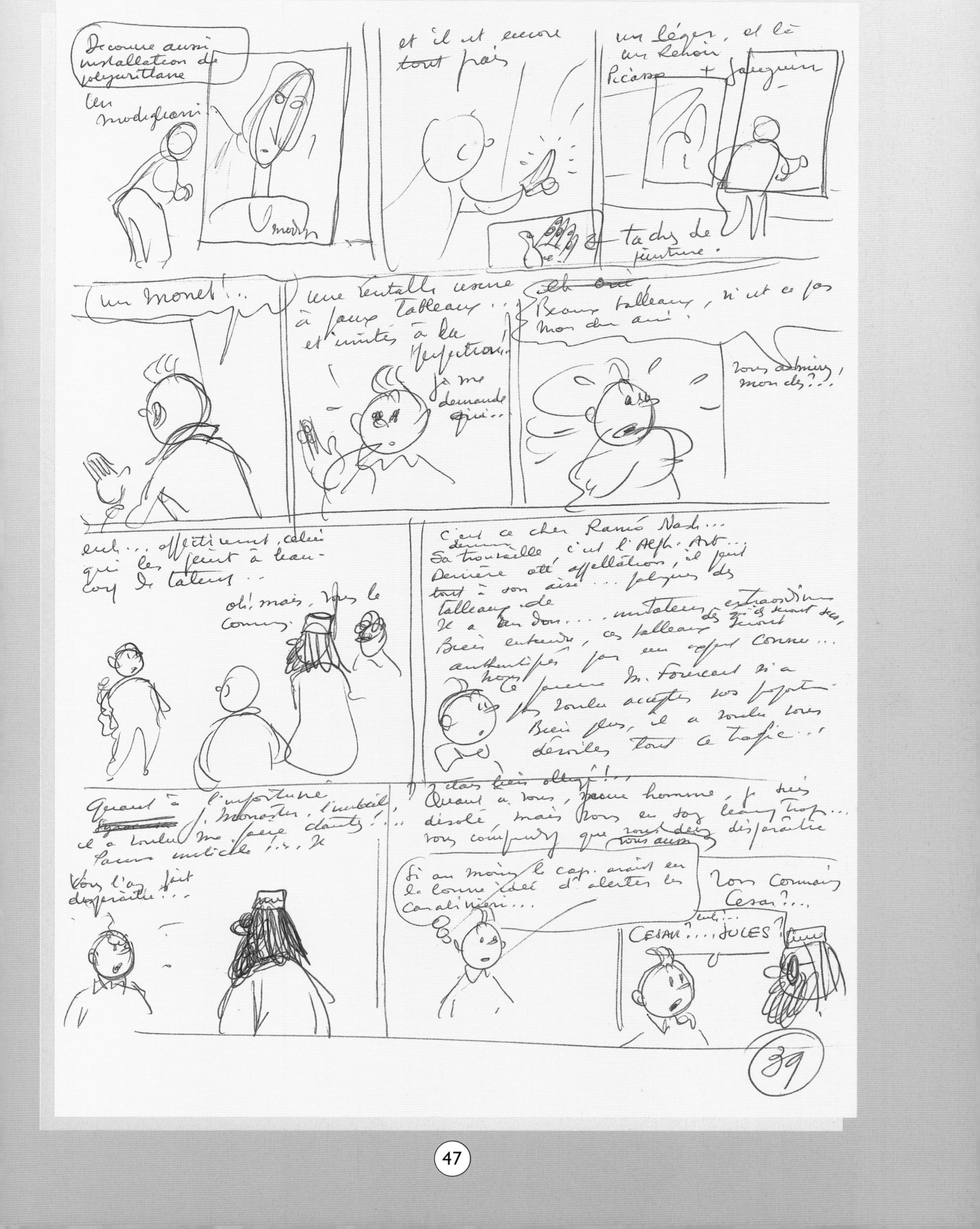

un Modigliani
et il est encore tout frais
un Léger, et là un Renoir
Picasso
taches de peinture.
un Monet!...
à faux tableaux...
je me demande qui...
Vous admirez, mon cher?...
oh! mais, vous le connaissez:
C'est ce cher Ramó Nash...
Sa trouvaille, c'est l'Alph-Art...
désolé, mais vous en savez beaucoup trop...
Si au moins le cap. avait eu la bonne idée d'alerter les carabiniers...
Vous connaissez César?...
CÉSAR?... JULES?
39

The final picture...

ENDADDINE: No, just César, the sculptor, the master of compressionism. Look, this is one of his. He's also an expansionist, as in this piece here… Well, my friend, we're going to pour liquid polyester over you; you'll become an expansion signed by César and then authenticated by a well-known expert. Then it will be sold, perhaps to a museum, or perhaps to a rich collector… You should be glad, your corpse will be displayed in a museum. And no one will ever suspect that the work, which could be entitled 'Reporter', constitutes the last resting place of young Tintin. Think about all that, my dear friend. Tomorrow, Ramó Nash will be here and will turn you into a 'César'!... Ha! Ha! Ha!... You there, take him away! And lock him up you-know-where…

A BODYGUARD *(pointing his gun)*: Come on, move!

Escorted by the two gorillas, Tintin is taken to a remote cell in the basement of the villa.

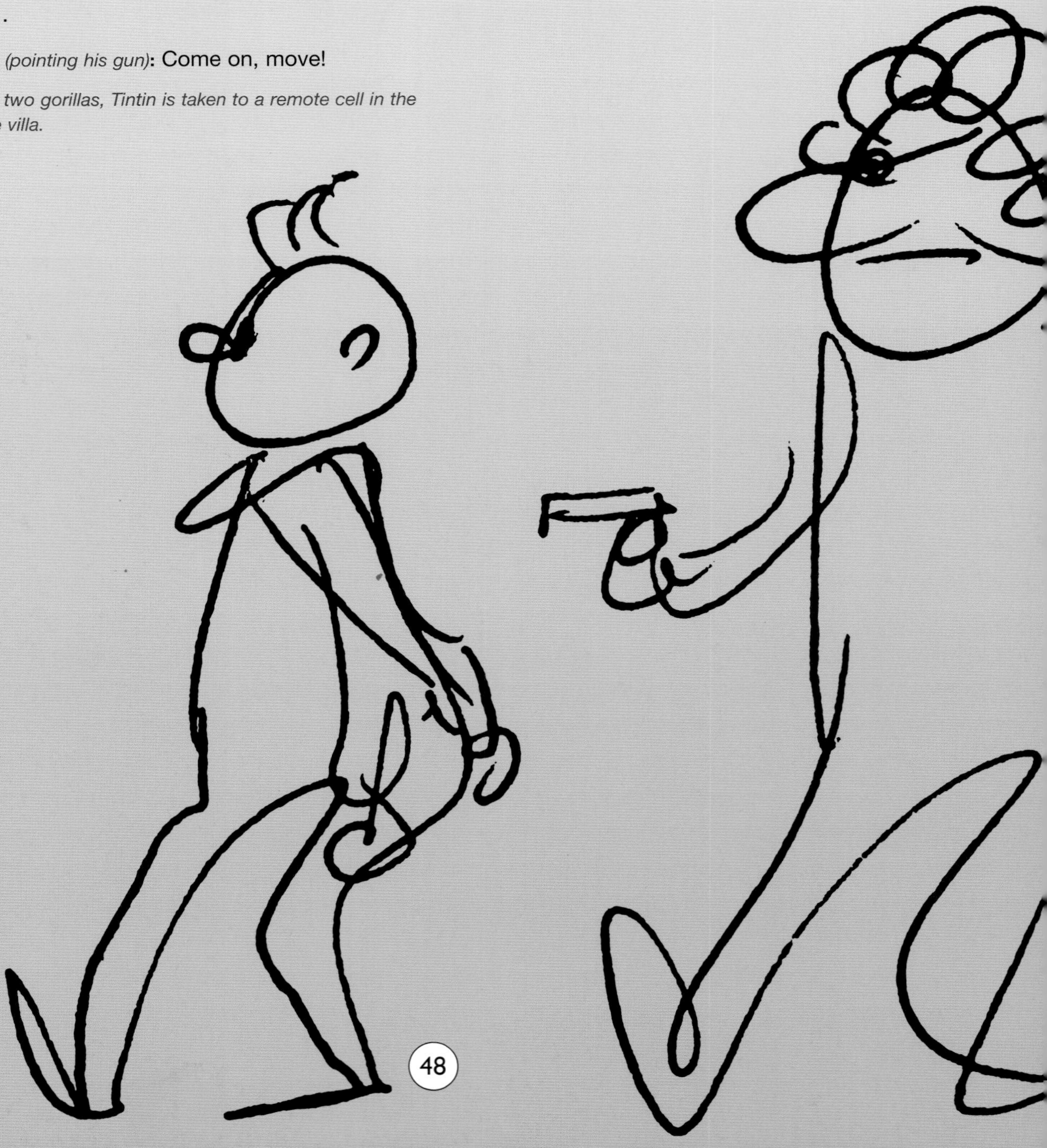

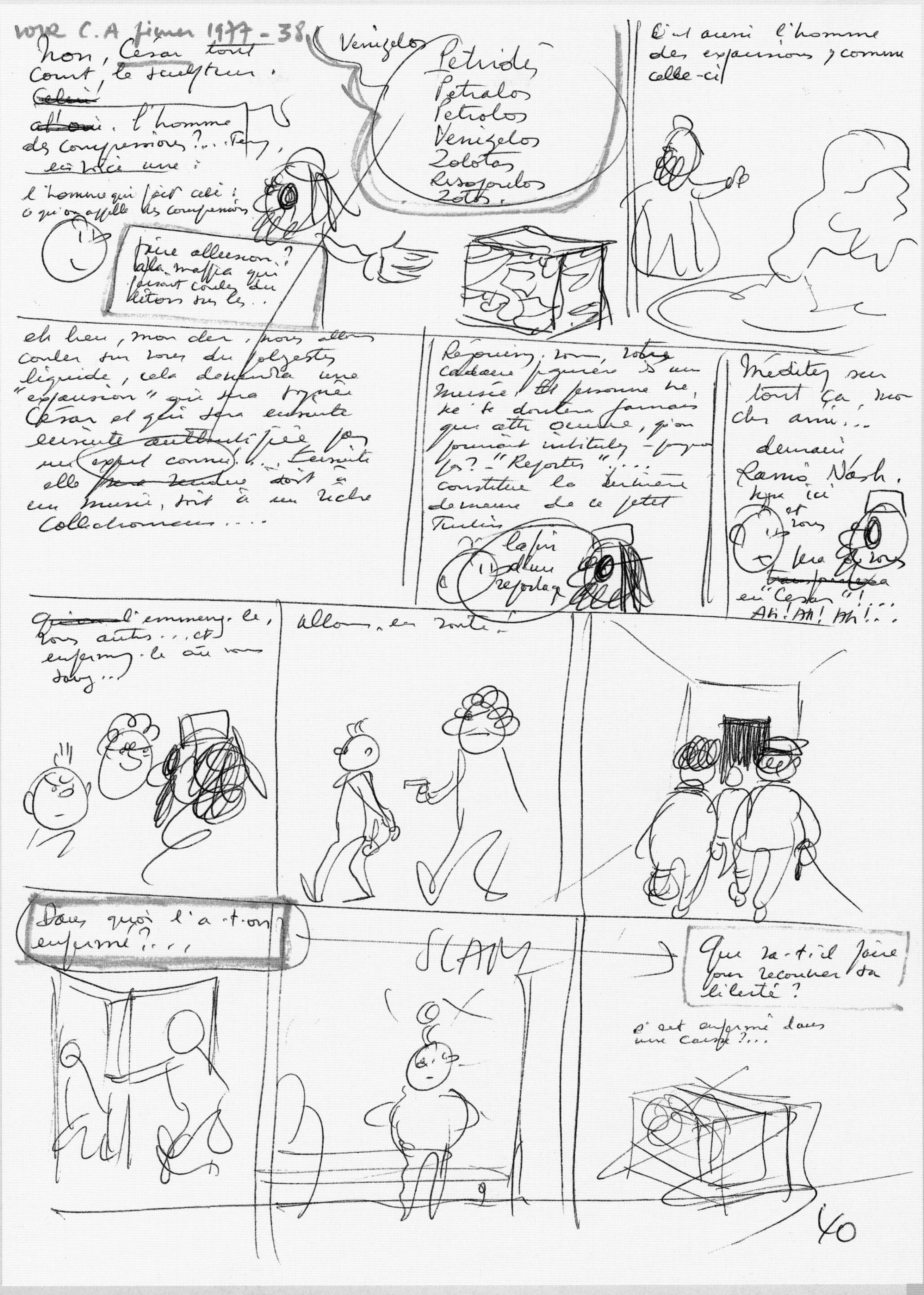

Non, César tout court, le sculpteur.
Pétridès
Petralos
Petrolos
Venizelos
Zolotas
D'ailleurs l'homme des expansions, comme celle-ci
Méditez sur tout ça, mon cher ami!...
Allons, en route!
Dans quoi l'a-t-on enfermé?...
SLAM
Que va-t-il faire pour recouvrer sa liberté?
s'est enfermé dans une caisse?...
40

TINTIN: How am I going to get out of it this time?

In a corner of the dungeon, Tintin sees some packing cases. Piling them up, he manages to climb to a ventilator protected by solid bars.

TINTIN: Help! Help! Rescue!

The grille in the cell door opens.

A VOICE: No use shouting, my young turkey-cock… No one can hear you.

Losing heart, Tintin crouches in a corner. But suddenly a faint noise makes him get up.

TINTIN: Snowy! … Wait, I'll give you a message to give to the Captain… To the Captain, understand?

Tintin scribbles a few words on a scrap of paper, folds it into four and throws it to Snowy. But the paper falls back. After several attempts, Snowy manages to seize the message and dash away.

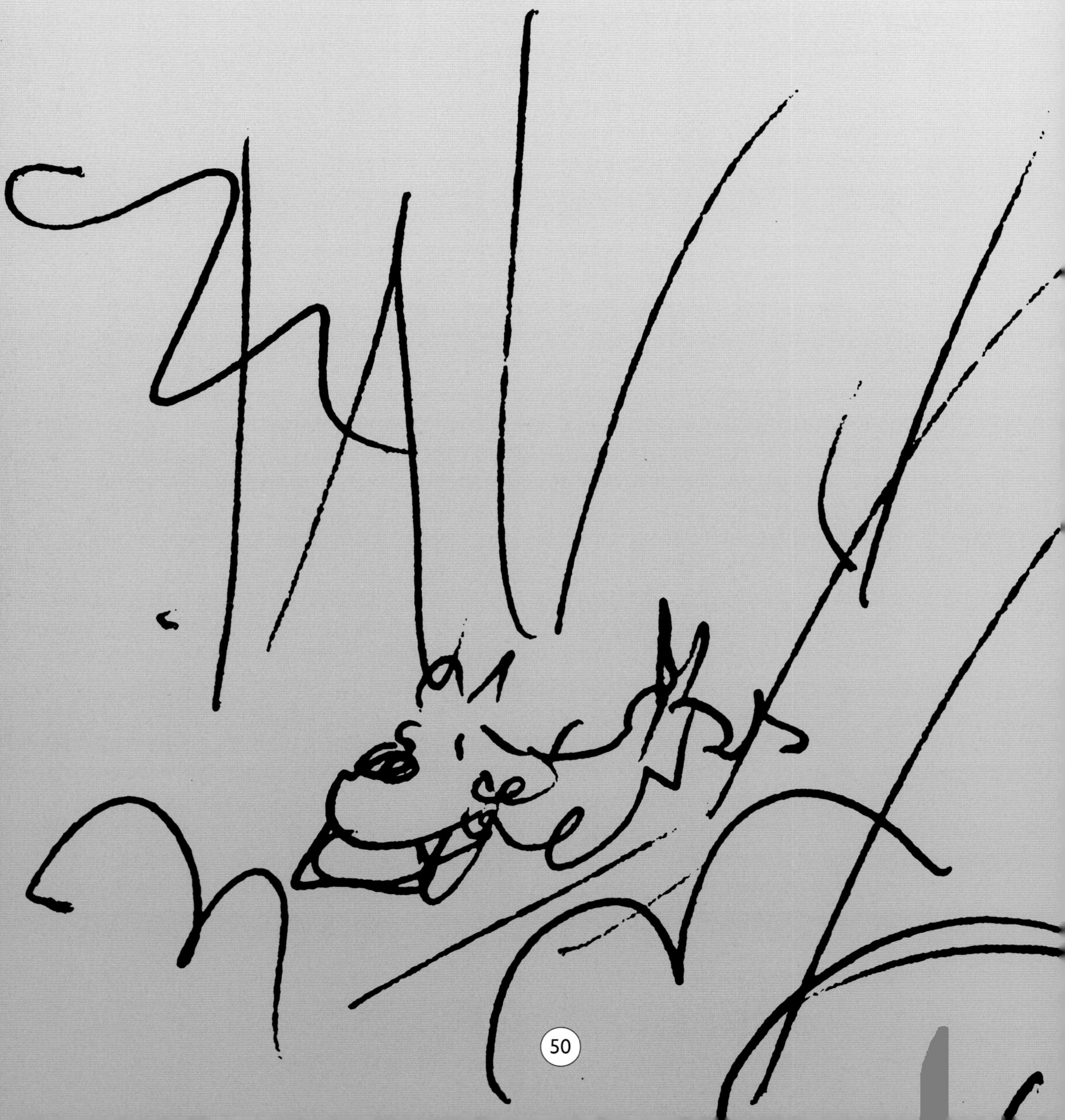

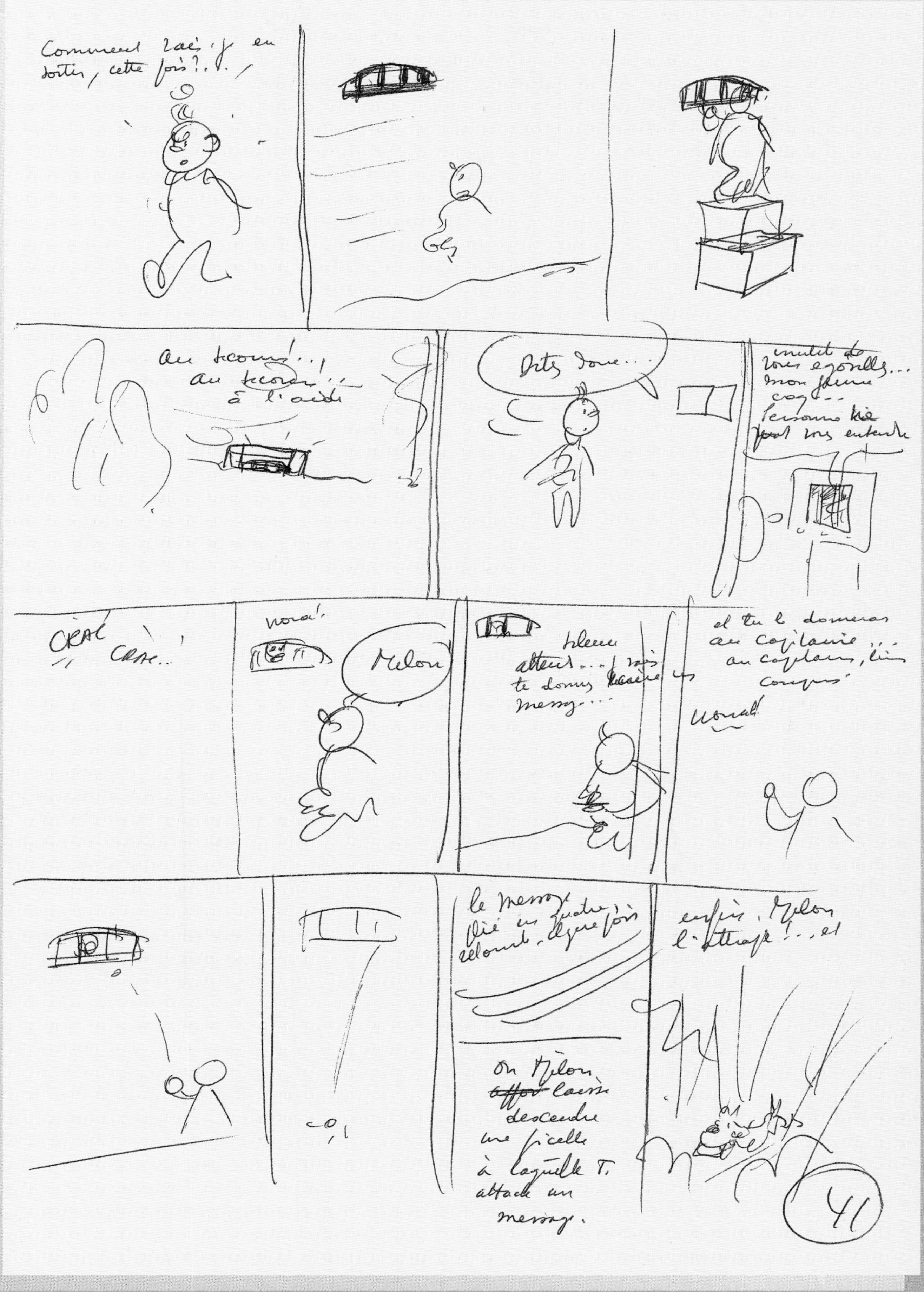
Comment vais-je en sortir, cette fois?..
au secours!.. au secours!.. à l'aide
Dites donc...
Inutile de vous égosiller... mon jeune coq... personne ne peut vous entendre
CRAC
CRAC...
Milou
et tu le donneras au capitaine, au capitaine, tu comprends
enfin, Milou l'attrape!... et
ou Milou laisse descendre une ficelle à laquelle T. attache un message.
41

The long night passes. Day breaks while Tintin is still asleep. The bodyguard awakens him roughly.

THE GUARD: On your feet! Get moving! It's time for you to be turned into a 'César'…

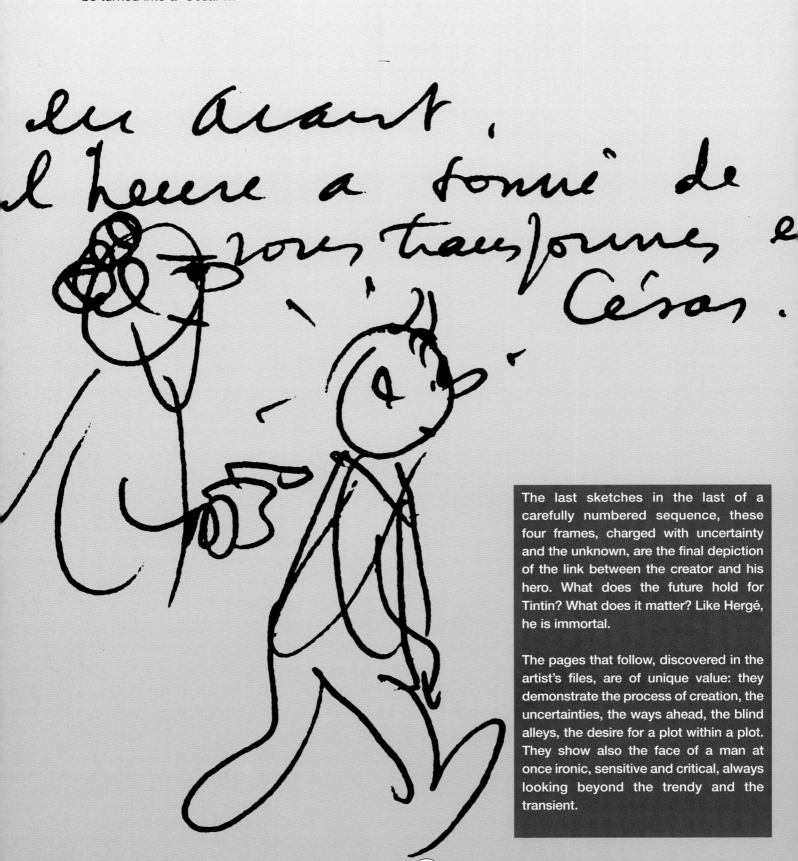

The last sketches in the last of a carefully numbered sequence, these four frames, charged with uncertainty and the unknown, are the final depiction of the link between the creator and his hero. What does the future hold for Tintin? What does it matter? Like Hergé, he is immortal.

The pages that follow, discovered in the artist's files, are of unique value: they demonstrate the process of creation, the uncertainties, the ways ahead, the blind alleys, the desire for a plot within a plot. They show also the face of a man at once ironic, sensitive and critical, always looking beyond the trendy and the transient.

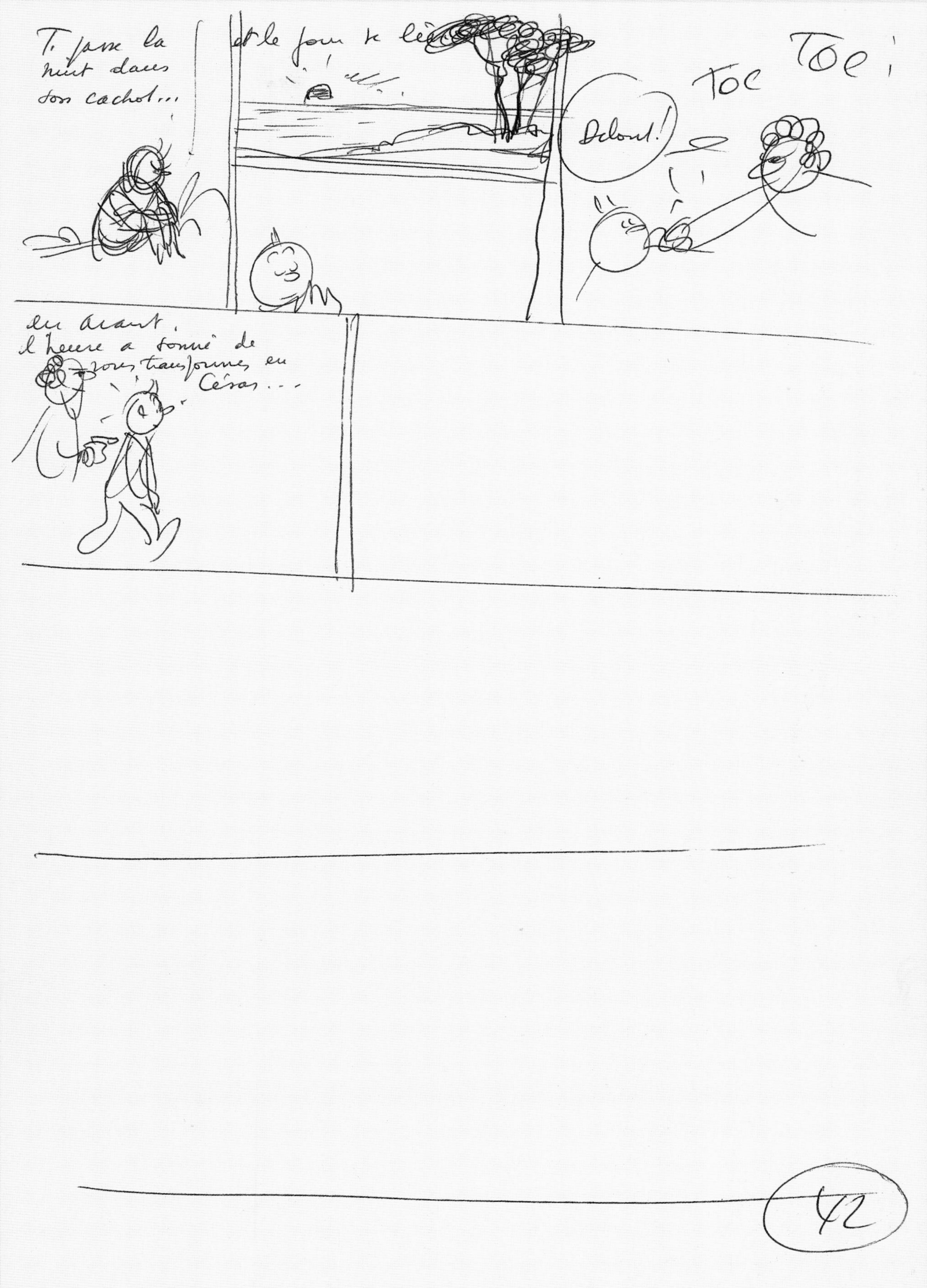
Ti passe la nuit dans son cachot...
et le jour se lè
Debout!
TOC
TOC!
En avant,
l'heure a sonné de vous transformer en César...
42

Rediscovered pages...

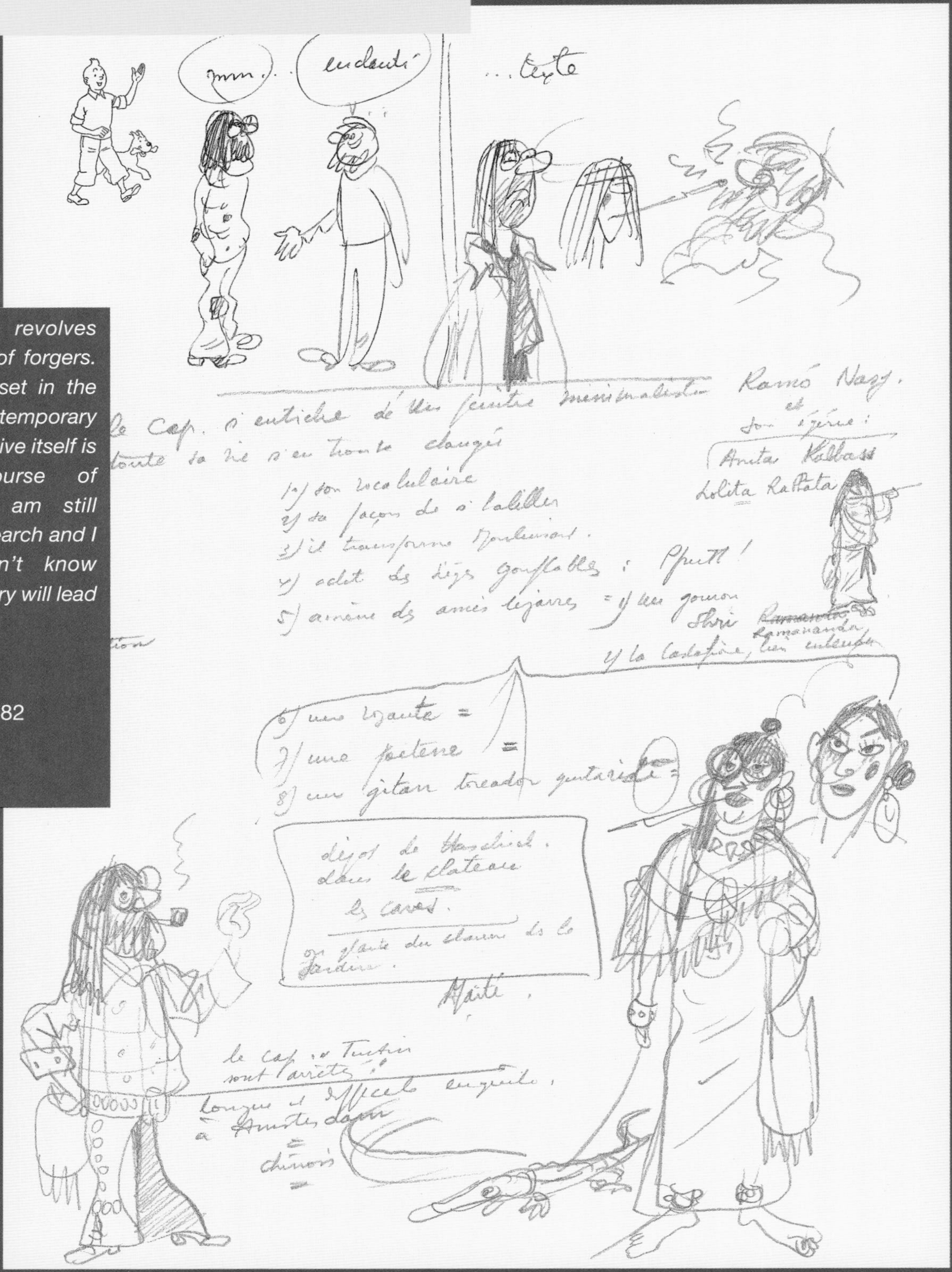

...texte
Lolita Raffata

'The story revolves round a tale of forgers. The book is set in the world of contemporary art. The narrative itself is in the course of evolution. I am still doing my research and I honestly don't know where this story will lead me...'

Hergé
December 1982

Another plot was explored, among traffickers in the field where Tintin forever does battle: drugs.

'The Captain is infatuated with a minimalist painter, Ramó Nash, and his life is changed: his vocabulary, his style of dress; he transforms the house, buys inflatable furniture, collects bizarre friends: a clairvoyante, a priestess, a gipsy bull-fighter… Hashish is stored in the cellars at Marlinspike, hemp planted in the gardens. The Captain and Tintin are arrested. A long and difficult investigation takes place in Amsterdam.'

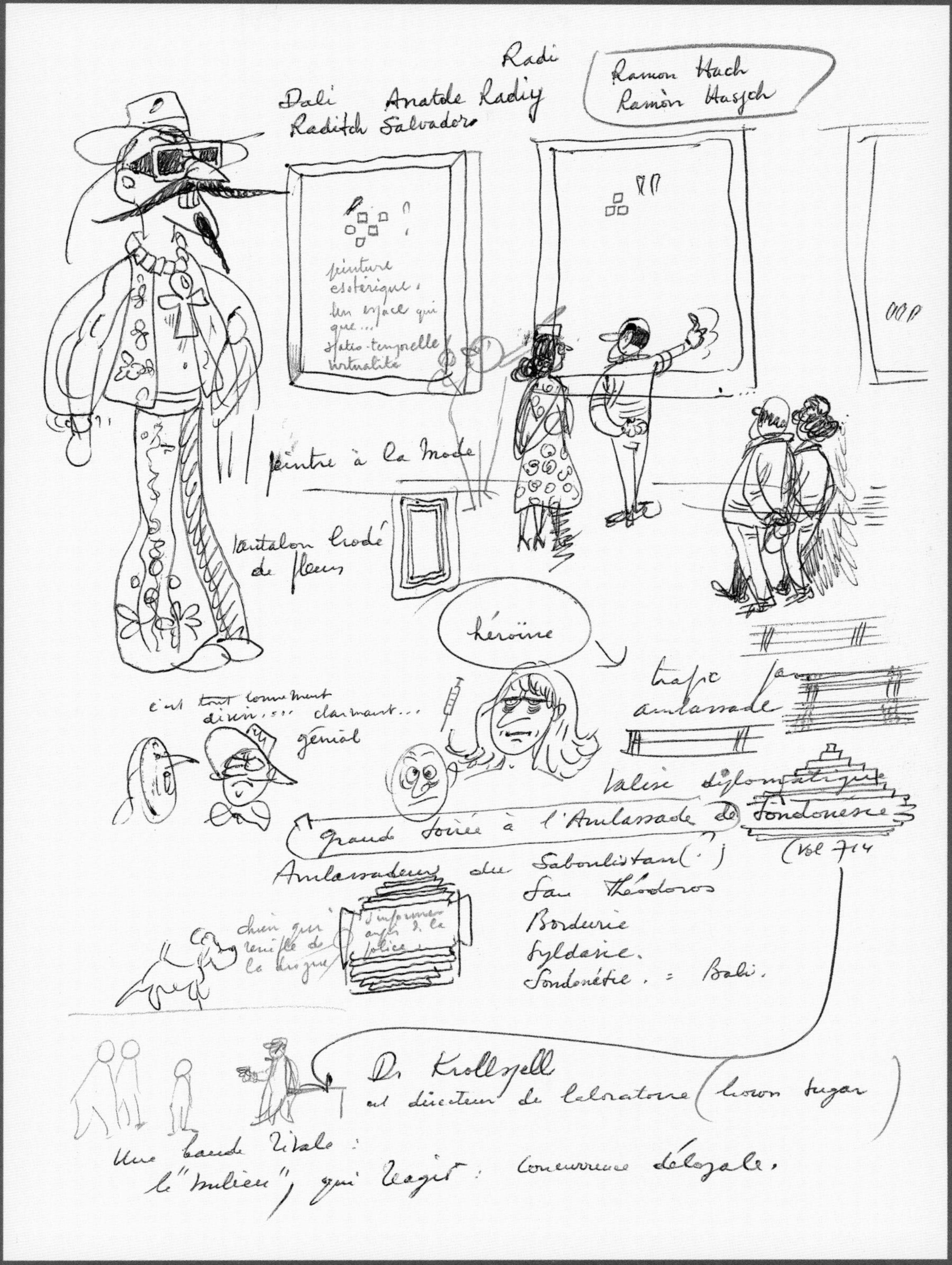
Dali
Radi
peinture à la mode
pantalon brodé de fleurs
héroïne
trafic par ambassade
valise diplomatique
San Théodoros
Bordurie
Syldavie
Dr Krollspell
concurrence déloyale.

Painting on the one hand: *'esoteric painting, spatial-temporal, virtuality, painting à la mode'*; narcotics on the other: *'heroin, trafficking in the embassy'*. Which embassy? Sondonesia, undoubtedly, where they receive at *'a grand soirée, the ambassadors of Saboulistan, San Theodoros, Borduria, Syldavia, and local worthies from Sondonesia'*. And Dr Krollspell reappears, having been *'director of a brown sugar laboratory'*. But a rival gang appears so that the *'underworld'* reacts in the face of this unfair competition.

Rediscovered pages...

Neurasthénique.
le critique d'art bien connu : Van Peteghem
Conscientisation
a perdu tous ses cheveux et sa barbe.
+ des taches sur le visage.
etc...
et le cap. retrouve le goût du whisky.

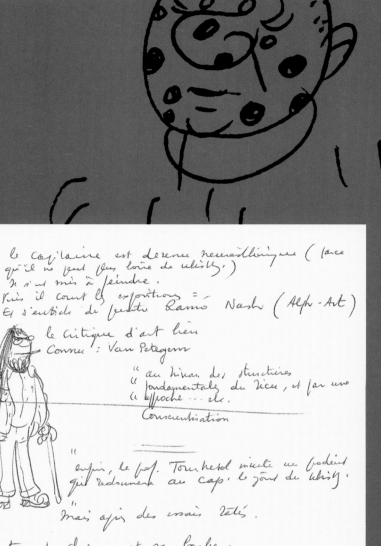

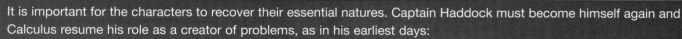

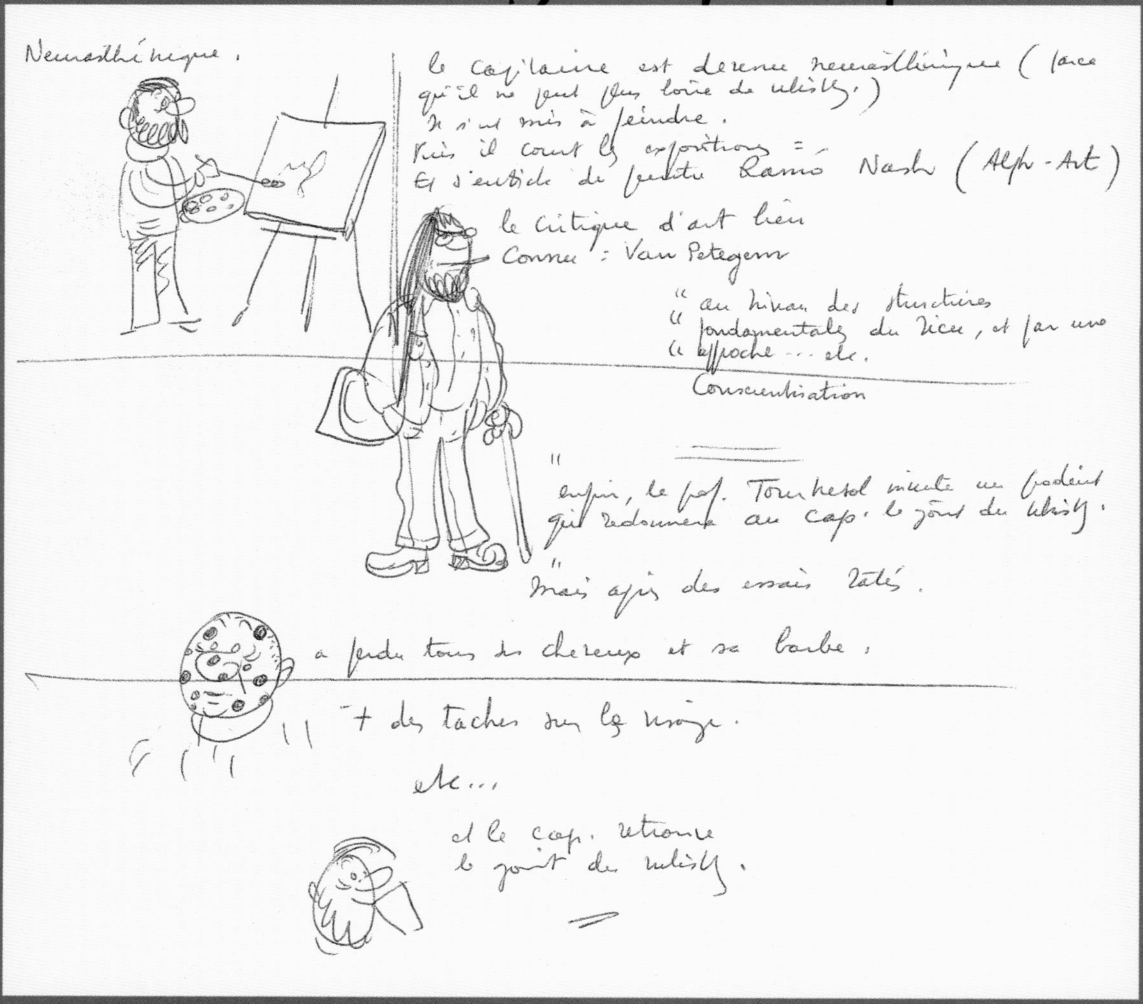

It is important for the characters to recover their essential natures. Captain Haddock must become himself again and Calculus resume his role as a creator of problems, as in his earliest days: *'The Captain has become neurasthenic (because he can no longer drink whisky). He has begun to paint. He scurries round the exhibitions and becomes infatuated with the painter Ramó Nash (Alph-Art).'* An art critic will discern something unusual in his work *'at the level of structures with the fundamentals of nothingness'*. And then *'at last Professor Calculus invents a product which restores the Captain's taste for whisky. But the failed attempts cost the Captain all his hair and his beard, with blotches on his face, etc. But the Captain recovers his taste for whisky.'*

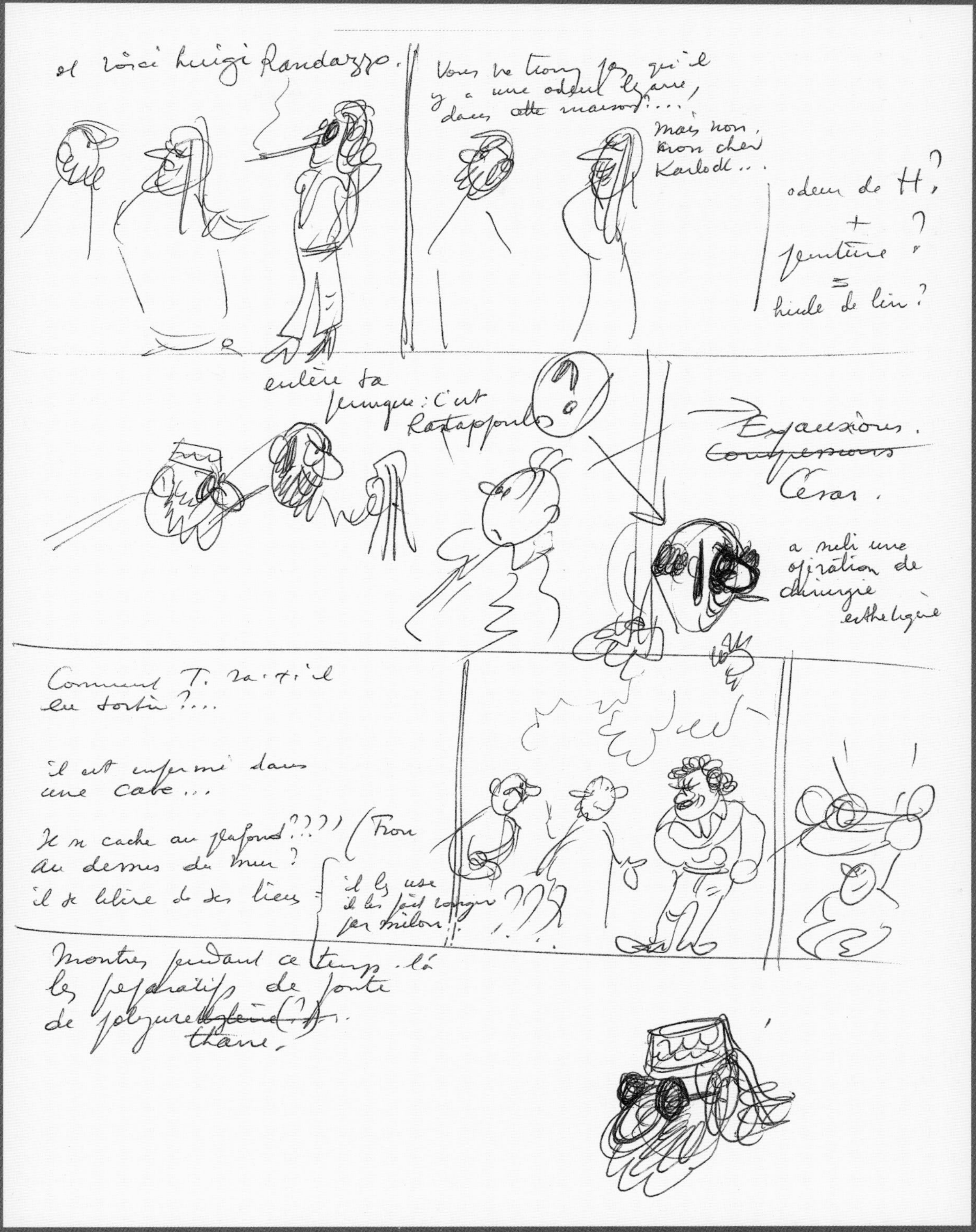

et voici Luigi Randazzo.
Vous ne trouvez pas qu'il y a une odeur bizarre, dans cette maison?...
Mais non, mon cher
César.
a subi une opération de chirurgie esthétique
Comment T. va-t-il en sortir?...
il est enfermé dans une cave...
Il se cache au plafond???? (Trou au dessous du mur?
il se libère de ses liens
il les use
il les fait ronger par Milou???
Montrer pendant ce temps-là les préparatifs de fonte de polyuréthane.

Suddenly, the ultimate enemy pops up, literally unmasked: plastic surgery only conceals half of Rastapopoulos, the worst of the worst. *'How will Tintin escape? He is imprisoned in a cellar, he hides in the ceiling (hole under the wall???). He frees himself from his bonds: he wears them away, he gets Snowy to bite them through???'* Meanwhile the *'polyurethane casting'* is being prepared.

Rediscovered pages...

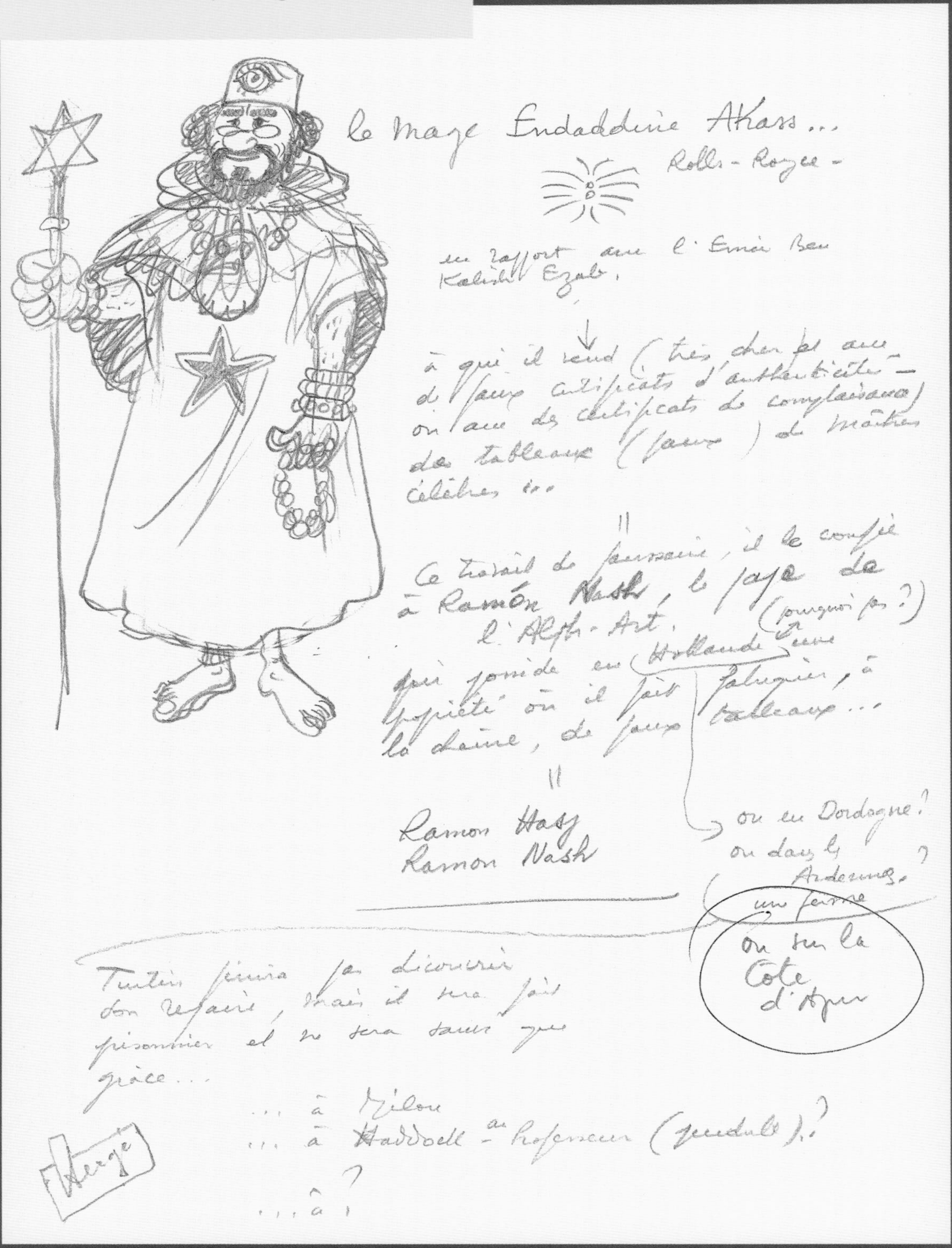
le Mage Endaddine Akass...
Rolls-Royce -
en rapport avec l'Emir Ben Kalish Ezab,
à qui il vend (très cher et avec de faux certificats d'authenticité – ou avec des certificats de complaisance) des tableaux (faux) de maîtres célèbres...
Ce travail de faussaire, il le confie à Ramón Nash, le pape de l'Alph-Art, (pourquoi pas?)
qui possède en Hollande une propriété où il fait fabriquer, à la chaîne, de faux tableaux...
ou en Dordogne? ou dans les Ardennes?
une ferme
ou sur la Côte d'Azur
Ramon Hash
Ramon Nash
Tintin finira par découvrir son repaire, mais il sera fait prisonnier et ne sera sauvé que grâce...
... à Milou
... à Haddock – au professeur (pendule)?
... à ?
Hergé

'The mystic Endaddine Akass (he travels in a Rolls Royce) is in touch with Emir Ben Kalish Ezab to whom he is selling (at a very high price and with false certificates of authenticity – or with certificates of accommodation) pictures (forged) by great masters… This work of forgery he entrusts to Ramón Nash, the high priest of Alph-Art (why not?), who owns in Holland (or in the Dordogne, or in the Ardennes, or on the Côte d'Azur) a property where he manufactures, on a production line, fake pictures.'

'Tintin ends up by discovering his hide-out, but he is taken prisoner and can only be saved thanks to… Snowy? Haddock? the Professor? To…?'

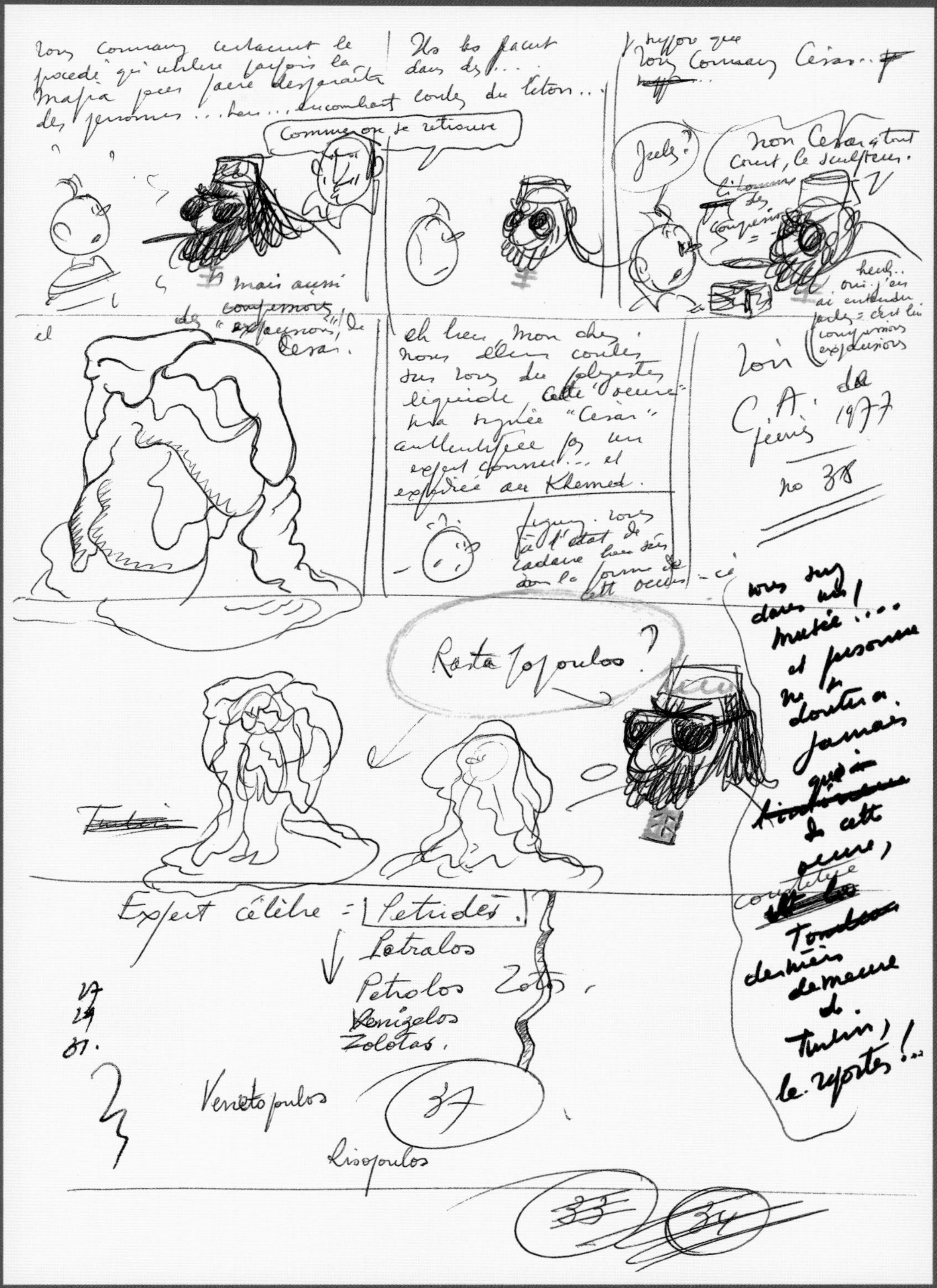
Rastapopoulos?
Expert célèbre = Petridès
Petralos
Petrolos Zotos
Venizelos
Zolotas.
Venetopulos
Lisopoulos
no 38
37
33
34

Tintin and Rastapopoulos have again come face to face: *'So we meet again!'* 'Well, my friend, we are going to pour liquid polyester over you. The work will be signed César and authenticated by a recognised expert… and sent to Khemed. You know César?' *'Julius?'* asks Tintin. *'No, César, the sculptor. You'll be in a museum!... And no one will ever know that the work constitutes the last resting-place of Tintin the reporter!'*

Rediscovered pages...

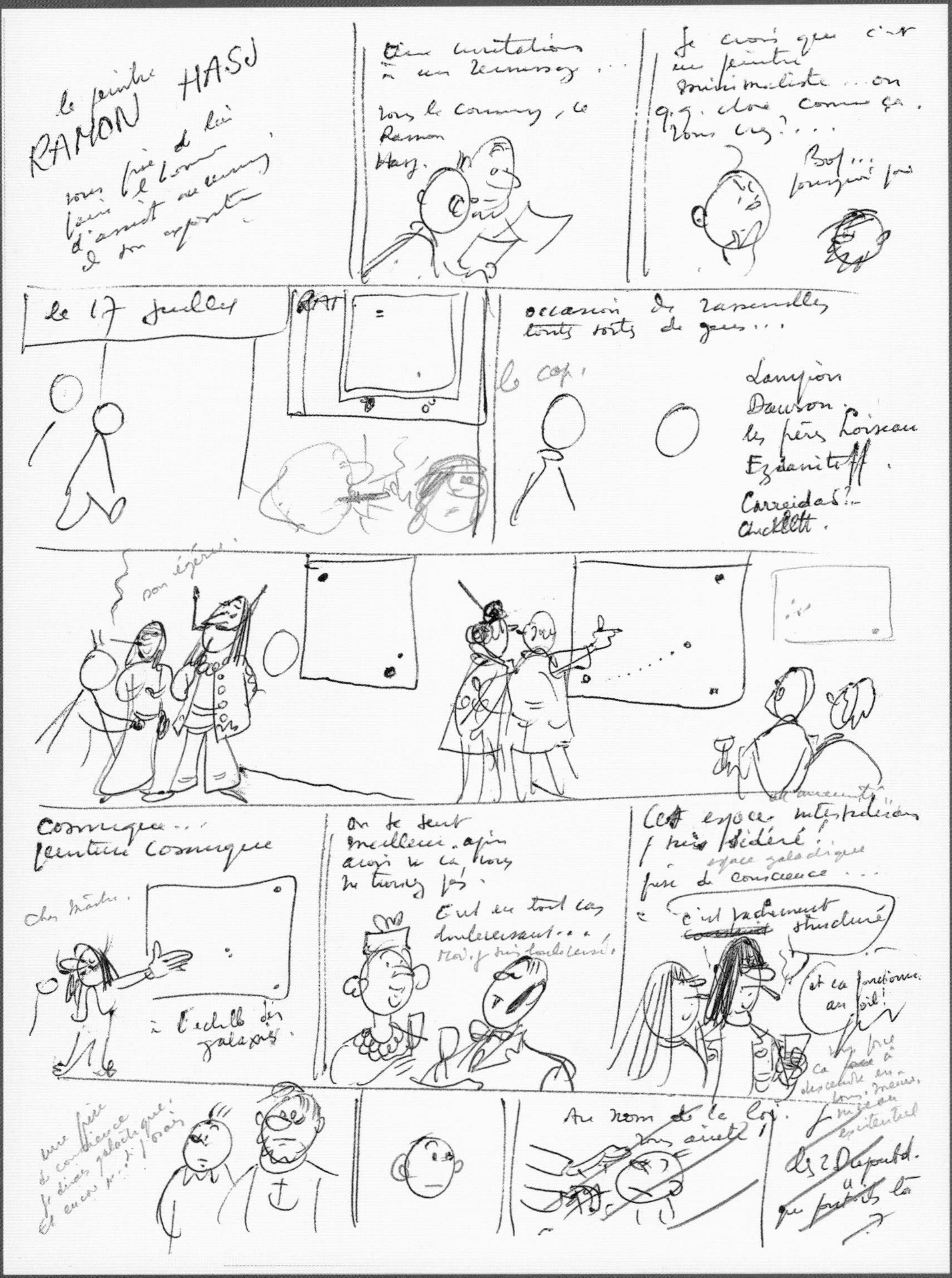
RAMON HASJ
Lampion
Dawson
Ezdanitoff
Carreidas?..
Au nom de la loi

Haddock is invited to the private view of an exhibition by Ramon Hasj, *'a minimalist painter, or something like that'*. An opportunity for the artist *'to assemble all sorts of people…'* and to collect old friends together in the story: *'Wagg, Dawson, the Bird brothers, Ezdanitoff, Carreidas, Trickler'*. An opportunity also to mock the pretensions and vanity of today's experts in the field of art: *'One feels better for seeing that, don't you think?' says one. 'It's simply stunning, and as for me, I'm stunned…'* says the other.

le capitaine fréquente
les milieux "artistes".
et fétiche de l'art actuel
achète sculptures peintures.
et un jour fait livrer une peinture à Moulinsart…
Tout change, l'intérieur, le décoration, les tableaux,
Hasj
Nhasj Nach
Hasj
Nasch
Nash
Ramó Nasj
Ramon Asj
Asj
Ajs Asj
Ramó Nasjch
Hasch
Hasj
Ram O'Nash
Ramon
Ramo Nash
une entité responsable de son cheminement

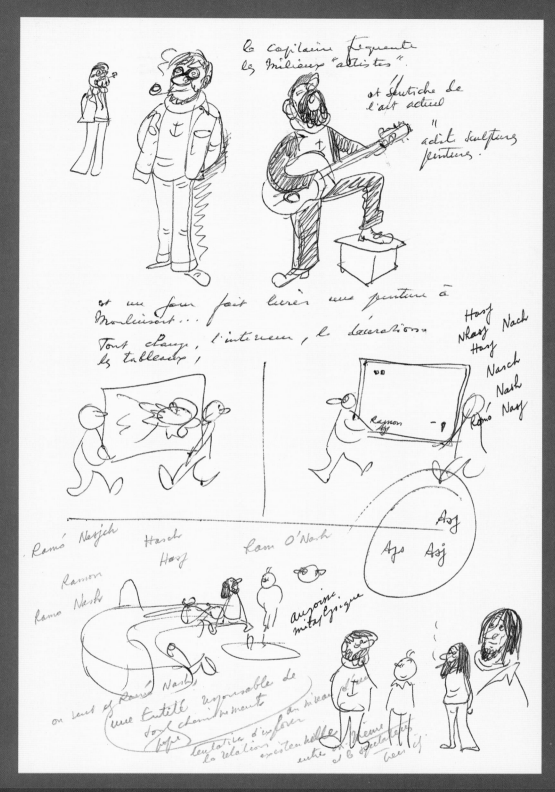

Hypothesis: the Captain has changed. *'He frequents "artistic" milieux, infatuated with today's art, he buys sculptures and paintings'*. He dresses differently, he sings, plays the guitar *'and, one day, has a painting delivered to Marlinspike… Everything changes, the interior, the décor, the pictures.'*

But, to come to the point, what indeed to call the painter? *'Hasj, Nhasj, Nach, Nasch, Nash, Nasj… Asg, Aje, Asj… Ramó Nasjch, Ramon Hasch or Hasj, Ramo Nash, Ram O'Nash?'* No matter, in him one senses *'an entity responsible for his own development'*. One can't say better than that…

Rediscovered pages…

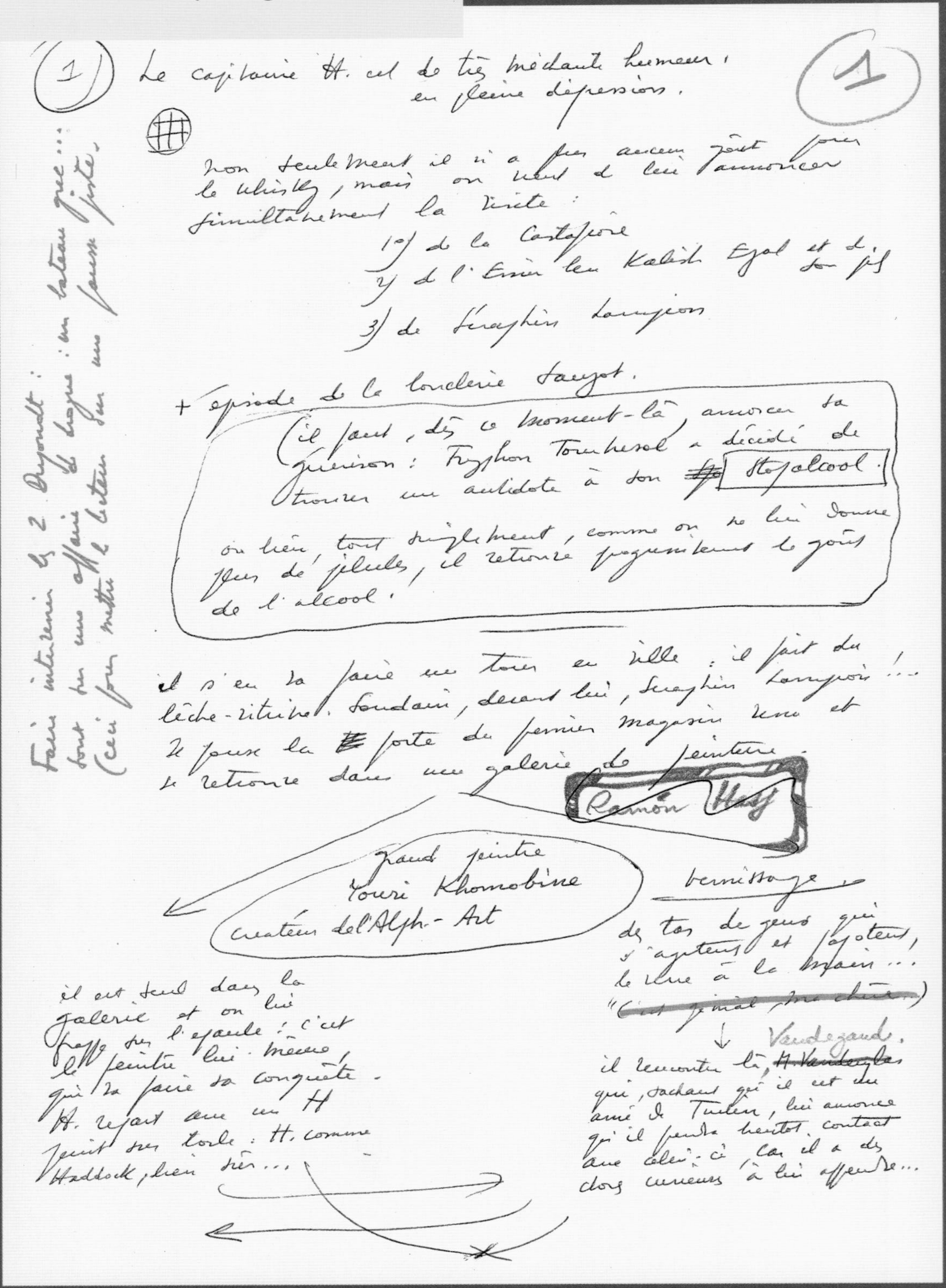
(1) Le capitaine H. est de très méchante humeur, en pleine dépression.

1

Non seulement il n'a plus aucun goût pour le whisky, mais on vient de lui annoncer simultanément la visite :
1°/ de la Castafiore
2/ de l'Emir ben Kalish Ezab et de son fils
3/ de Séraphin Lampion

+ épisode de la boucherie Sanzot.

(il faut, dès ce moment-là, amorcer sa guérison : Tryphon Tournesol a décidé de trouver un antidote à son Stopalcool.

ou bien, tout simplement, comme on ne lui donne plus de pilules, il retrouve progressivement le goût de l'alcool.

il s'en va faire un tour en ville : il fait du lèche-vitrines. Soudain, devant lui, Séraphin Lampion !... Il pousse la porte du premier magasin venu et se retrouve dans une galerie de peinture.

grand peintre
Youri Khomobine
créateur de l'Alph-Art

vernissage :
des tas de gens qui s'agitent et papotent, le verre à la main...
("C'est génial ma chère")

il rencontre là, Vandezande qui, sachant qu'il est un ami de Tintin, lui annonce qu'il prendra bientôt contact avec celui-ci car il a des choses curieuses à lui apprendre...

il est seul dans la galerie et on lui frappe sur l'épaule : c'est le peintre lui-même, qui va faire sa conquête. H. repart avec un H peint sur toile : H. comme Haddock, bien sûr...

Faire intervenir les 2 Dupondt : tout sur une affaire de drogues : un bateau que... (ceci pour mettre le lecteur sur une fausse piste)

Hergé certainly makes up his mind about Haddock. *'Captain H. is in a very bad mood, thoroughly depressed. Not only has he no longer any taste for whisky, he has just heard that he is about to be visited by La Castafiore, by Emir Ben Kalish Ezab and his son, and by Jolyon Wagg.'* To confuse the reader, the Thompsons are inquiring into *'a case involving drugs'*, *'a ship that…'*. Calculus is seeking an antidote for Stopalcool, Cutts the butcher elbows his way into the narrative. Haddock *'goes for a stroll in the town'*, sees Jolyon Wagg, dives into an art gallery where the director has secrets for Tintin…

Haddock *'is alone in the gallery when someone taps him on the shoulder: it is the painter himself who is going to make a conquest'*. *'H. leaves with an H painted on canvas. H. as in Haddock, of course…'*